The RESURRECTION *Encounter*

The RESURRECTION *Encounter*

A Science Fiction Parable for a Nuclear Age

Tom T. Skore

Printed in the United States of America
ISBN 978-1-967279-75-3 (hc)
ISBN 978-1-967279-73-9 (sc)
ISBN 978-1-967279-74-6 (e)

2026.02.12

This book is printed on acid-free paper.

Blue Ink Media Solutions
1111B S Governors Ave
STE 7582 Dover,
DE 19904

www.blueinkmediasolutions.com

DEDICATION

Dedicated to my late wife, Dayle Diane Hilborn Skore, the single greatest influence in my life, without whose encouragement I would never have begun writing.

I also wish to thank my current partner, Ila Jean Skore, who has so lovingly supported all my efforts over the past twenty-six years and made life worth living once again.

Table of Contents

CHAPTER 1

The vessel had been in geostationary orbit over the eastern Mediterranean for six months when the landing party first saw him. The aliens had been gathering food, water, and other supplies in an effort to restock their ship. It was always difficult to know just when they would find another suitable planet.

Nor were the proper supplies easy to find. Crude farming techniques made for foods which lacked abundant nutrients, making their synthesizer's job much more difficult as it distilled the bulky materials down into easily storable tablets. Metals were imperfect, their assortment limited, so raw ores needed to be located for conversion into the alloys that the aliens needed for refitting their advanced electronics. Nor were those the only problems.

They didn't mind, however, because they found Earth particularly beautiful. Rich blue skies and green oceans, magnificent cloud formations, and varied topography, all made the thought of leaving painful. Not many places like this existed in the galaxies they had traveled. It made them long for the home to which they could never return.

As for Earth's inhabitants, they were one of the most interesting, yet volatile species the aliens had encountered. Humans showed incredible promise, but had a long journey ahead. They were at a crossroads when the man called Jesus entered their world.

Kaseel was the first of the crew to come into contact with him. He was the youngest of the aliens, though the distinction was dubious. So much time was spent in stasis while the ship traveled at speeds approaching light that, by his planet's standards, Kaseel was millions of years old.

He was a formidable scientist who was familiar with all the ship's systems. This made him a likely choice for the assignment of gathering supplies and information, but it could be argued that all of the aliens possessed knowledge sufficient for the job. They were an order of traveling scientists, each with a particular area of expertise, but all were well versed in the fundamental operations of the ship.

What made Kaseel particularly well suited for the assignment was his height. At a meter and a half, a giant by his peoples' standards, he was the one who passed most easily as a human. Even at that, it required that he remain bundled in a cloak to hide his slightly grayish skin, hairless head, and distinctive, other-worldly features. In his favor, abnormalities were common during these times, and many people were disfigured by disease. The few people who got a close look at him just moved away. But Kaseel had to be careful. Fear was everywhere. Should he be labeled a leper, or any other type of social pariah, the entire mission would be compromised.

The aliens were small and rather delicate creatures, and Kaseel's missions were very fatiguing. Earth's gravitational field and oxygen levels took weeks to adapt to, as did the intense heat of the sun, so direct and close in proximity. The fact that he needed to stay fully covered made the heat even more oppressive at first, but once he was acclimatized, he began to enjoy the outings. He often felt sorry for his shipmates, still confined to the vessel.

On rare occasions, Shule, another alien nearly Kaseel's size would accompany him. But if there was not a specific need it was felt that exposure should be limited, and Kaseel was the one on call.

Those who remained on board explored the planet and its inhabitants through the lenses of micro cameras carried within the folds of Kaseel's specially designed cloak. A few times Kaseel took one of the portable holographic scanner/projectors, but there were trade-offs. While the device was a valuable research tool, allowing them to create an extensive library of three-dimensional images of the animals, plants, and artifacts they found throughout the galaxies, its size made it difficult to conceal; thus there was always the possibility of discovery.

Kaseel's shipmates functioned as an extended brain for him, as near as the amplifier planted in his ear. They provided him with technical data and advice, feeding information into the computers and getting it back to Kaseel in a timely manner so he never felt alone.

By this time all seven crew members were becoming reasonably familiar with several of Earth's tongues. Sample recordings were analyzed by the computers and little-by-little the gaps in their understanding began to disappear. Their own language was far more complex, and their aptitude for acquiring new languages was extremely acute after years of space travel and contact with other species. The timing was perfect. Had their efforts to decipher Aramaic, or any one of a dozen other factors not occurred at precisely that time, the man's words may have gone unnoticed by the aliens altogether.

Kaseel couldn't quite put his finger on what was different about this man called Jesus. There was a quiet strength in his demeanor, a wonderful combination of gentleness and intensity which drew Kaseel to him, along with throngs of humans. But there was something intangible that defied understanding. And while Jesus spoke of peace and love, it was clear that he had the courage and conviction to stand in opposition to all who sought to block his message.

People spoke of miracles, some insisting that he was their Messiah, or Savior. This he did not understand. Neither had Kaseel ever seen one of these miracles, though it made little difference to him, for the man's words resonated with good will, and common sense dictated compliance with little need for proof. The ideals the man called Jesus preached about reminded Kaseel of the philosophies of his own people, but the notion of God and faith, believing in something essentially unprovable, was new and strange.

CHAPTER 2

Shortly after Kaseel first heard Jesus speak, it became apparent Jesus was in danger. It seemed strange to the aliens that messages of peace could be considered seditious, and could in any way threaten the powers with their legions of soldiers. Yet it was clear trouble was imminent. It was also clear this man was not going to mollify his message.

A unanimous decision was made by the ship's crew to plant a locater on Jesus so they could keep track of his whereabouts. In addition, it would afford them the luxury of hearing every word he spoke. The transponder, no bigger than a tick, would be very hard for anyone to detect, especially in a world devoid of technology.

On the day of the plant Kaseel found Jesus speaking to a huge crowd. When finished, Jesus was stopped by admirers who were unwilling to let him leave. With patience and understanding he touched and spoke briefly with each one, smiling warmly before moving on to the next.

Kaseel waited on the periphery, not wanting to take the chance of exposure, nor daring to risk injury by the rambunctious crowd. He kept his face toward the ground, glancing up only occasionally to see how many were left. As the last of the people dispersed, he sensed Jesus looking at him, and then begin to move in his direction. Kaseel's heart began to race. In his ear, voices from the ship urged him to remain calm as they monitored his pulse.

Jesus reached out and touched Kaseel's shoulder, raising the alien's chin with his other hand. He looked straight into the alien's eyes, and from that moment on, Kaseel was his. Whether or not the man had noticed the alien's unusual features, Kaseel could not tell. If he had, he certainly never let on, and it certainly made no difference.

Suddenly Kaseel remembered what it was he was supposed to be doing. Dropping to the ground he kissed the hem of Jesus' robe while securing the locater to the cloth. The man reached down and pulled the alien up. He paused to study the alien's eyes for several seconds, smiled gently, then continued on his way.

The locater had been attached, and from that moment on, life on the ship would never be the same.

CHAPTER 3

They followed Jesus for months, finding goodness in every word he spoke. Then suddenly things turned even darker. Why it came to pass, the aliens never fully comprehended. The politics and hatred were beyond them. They were not strangers to pain or suffering, but in their world those things had always come as a result of natural causes, never inflicted by members of their own society. Yet here was a man who spoke of nothing but goodness, trying to end the suffering of his own kind, being hunted down like a criminal for his efforts.

It was in a place called Gethsemane that the magnitude of Jesus' burden became heartbreakingly clear to the aliens. Though they could not fathom the particulars, there was no denying Jesus' anguish, an anguish more profound than any of the aliens had ever witnessed. Though there was no way for Jesus to know anyone was listening, the aliens began to feel like interlopers. They monitored events in the Garden for only a short time before turning off the communication signal, giving Jesus privacy with his Father, and three disciples.

Had they overheard everything that transpired in the Garden that night they might have understood the Atonement, and its importance to Jesus, and thus, not intervened. Instead, as the possibility of execution moved swiftly toward actuality, all on board agreed that they must do something. The question was what?

Kaseel, who had been pondering the situation for some time, was the first to put forth a plan. His idea was bold, and the usually congenial group experienced some discord as they considered the details, and weighed the risks. Several times during the course of their discussions they came close to rejecting the idea altogether, but between their altruism, and the memory of Jesus' tormented voice in Gethsemane, the thought of abandoning him and reversing course was ultimately unthinkable.

That is how Kaseel found himself at the base of the hill that day, protecting his eyes from the ferocious wind whipping the dust. How difficult it had been not to intervene as they paraded Jesus through the streets, and hammered nails into his body. How many would have to suffer this way before the insanity would stop?

Kaseel positioned himself to one side of a small group of mourners holding vigil. Four Roman soldiers played a game called knucklebones on the back side of the hill, oblivious to the suffering so near to them on the crosses. The alien looked around nervously, biding his time, waiting for opportunity to present itself. His head snapped back around when he heard Jesus cry out in a desperate attempt to lift himself up to breathe.

Kaseel could wait no longer. He ran past the crowd and rushed up the hill. Wrapping his fragile arms around Jesus' blood stained legs he quickly injected a substance into Jesus' calf with a small, sophisticated appliance. An anesthetic, the compound would also significantly increase the blood's oxygen absorption levels, perhaps fooling the Romans, while buying the aliens a few precious minutes.

By the time the centurion became aware of Kaseel's presence and pushed him away with a harsh jab from his spear, the deed was finished. Kaseel picked himself up and moved back, the centurion completely unaware of what Kaseel had done.

In the ship's control room the other aliens breathed an audible sigh of relief. They had been standing in front of the communications console, watching the proceedings on one of the displays in silence. Volk, the control room wizard, ran his fingers across the surface of lights, touching several controls as he brought the centurion into tighter focus, adjusting for Kaseel's new position.

The centurion looked up at Jesus and studied his face. If this "Son of God" was still alive, he showed no outward signs. The centurion turned to the others: "It's time." The soldiers stopped their game and gathered up their amusements.

The aliens turned away from the display screen and glanced nervously at one another. From other crucifixions they had witnessed, this was often the most barbaric moment, and they were dreading it. When they looked back, their fears were substantiated. The soldiers were breaking the knees of the two flanking prisoners with large wooden hammers in an effort to hasten asphyxiation.

The centurion with the spear looked up at the center cross one last time. Then with a brutal thrust, he pierced Jesus' side.

Kaseel dropped his hood and headed toward the pick up point. Dark clouds were moving in quickly.

When night came two soldiers stood guard in front of the tomb, its huge round stone already in place. It was a quiet night, serene, with a sky full of stars, a welcome contrast to the violent storms that had punished the land during the afternoon.

Suddenly the soldiers became aware of an incredibly bright light coming from within the tomb. The light illuminated the outer edges of the stone, casting a halo over the surrounding terrain.

They rushed to push the stone aside, desperately trying to rock it back and forth. Once they had built enough momentum, it gave way and lifted out of its groove. Exhausted and out of breath, the soldiers peered into the gaping hole. All that was left was a piece of white linen, and the faintest trace of shimmering light.

CHAPTER 4

The ship's life functions center was a sterile environment bathed in soft blue light. Colorful readout displays provided an array of steady rhythmic beeps which covered the low drone of the ship. The stasis chambers used by the crew during interstellar travel lined the walls. All were empty and in their vertical positions save one which was down from the wall, open and horizontal. In it lay Jesus.

The substance which Kaseel had injected on the planet's surface had done its job. Though Jesus' heart had stopped beating before being brought aboard the ship, he had not been dead nearly as long as the Romans, or his followers had supposed. His injuries were severe, but luck had been on the aliens' side. They had succeeded in reviving him, but just barely.

Liam and Thelis, the ship's medical specialists were working feverishly to keep him that way. Jesus had been placed on a respirator. An electronic pump circulated his blood while the doctors struggled to repair damage to the heart itself.

Shafus, a doctor in his own right, was responsible for the crew's mental well being. He stood to one side, providing any needed assistance, be it an extra pair of hands, a drink of water for the surgeons, or simply an encouraging word.

The doctors were now in the process of reattaching the heart. It was a tense situation. Though their medical knowledge was vast, they knew that even in cases where there were striking similarities to other species, there were always subtle differences as well. In this case, caution had to be balanced with practicality, and speed.

Shafus kept close watch on the display readouts as the two surgeons neared completion of the delicate procedure. Every now and then he would glance at Jesus' face.

"He looks in pain even while he sleeps."

"Is it any wonder?" Thelis answered, remaining focused on his task.

Liam paid little attention to the exchange as he continued working. Finally, he let out a sigh and looked to Thelis. "You can cauterize those with the small beam now." He glanced over at Shafus. "His heart is beating, but I don't know if we can save him. He's lost a lot of blood, and it's nothing like ours."

"All you can do is your best," Shafus replied, reassuring Liam with a gentle touch on the shoulder. "Keep Mance and me updated."

Liam nodded as Shafus left the bay.

Mance was the ship's coordinator. The term had been specifically chosen so as not to link it with any kind of rank or power. Yet it was clear that all on board had a deep, abiding respect for this individual. And though never publicly stated, the crew tendered him command authority, trusting his decisions implicitly.

There was good reason for this. Mance had a brilliant mind, and a generous spirit. He was warm and efficient, humorous, with barely a trace of ego. And he was practical, always able to see a problem clearly, and perceive the appropriate course of action. Nor was he afraid of danger, if that was the only way. He was the heartbeat of the crew, without ever really being aware of it. The perfect leader, though he would contend, he had the perfect crew, and he probably would not have been far from wrong.

This mutual respect was a testament to the way the ship functioned, and to their cultural upbringing. It was a good thing, for they would be living out the rest of their lives in this fashion. There would be no going back.

Volk on the other hand was more of a pure scientist, with fewer social skills. It wasn't that he wasn't capable of them, he just didn't see the need for it. That was Mance's job as far as Volk was concerned. His job was to provide the steady stream of technical answers—to keep the data flowing. He knew the ship, and all on board were awed by his ability to make the complex look easy. He had a childlike fascination for gadgetry, but nothing could mask his competence.

Shule, the alien who would sometimes accompany Kaseel to the surface of the planet, had become the ship's jack-of-all-trades. He started the journey as a kind of space apprentice. It was thought his skills would then be put to use on another ship. Who could have anticipated how soon the end came. But Shule's good nature made the situation easy, and he found a comfortable niche over the years. The crew could not imagine life without him.

The three aliens were in the ship's science lab. The room was outfitted with computers, spectrometers, microscopes, holographic devices, and other varied appliances used for scientific research and the recording of data. Research and discovery was the ship's designated mission, which the crew pursued vigorously, not only because of their natural curiosity, but as a means of keeping their minds occupied. The ship had been designed for speed, with not a hint of weaponry, though the crew was quite capable of throwing something together if their survival should depend on it. That necessity, however, never came up.

It had been three days since the crucifixion, and Mance and Volk were busy creating a holographic interface with full range of motion. Shule's presence was merely cosmetic: he was modeling a flowing white shift.

The door to the lab opened and Shafus entered. "I have an image of his face on the portable."

He set the hand-held holographic scanner/projector on the computer's console where Volk proceeded to download the images. With the touch of a few more lights on the center console Volk had the ship's larger holographic scanner circling Shule in the center of the room. After several sweeps Volk looked over at Mance.

"Take a look."

Mance moved to the console display. He watched as Volk manipulated the images, combining Jesus' face with the scans of Shule, just as the alien now appeared in the center of the room. Little-by-little the two images began to merge.

"What do you think?" Volk said proudly, looking up at Mance.

"Needs to be taller," Mance responded, glancing back at Shule as if to check on his appraisal. It didn't help. Shule looked nothing like the image now. Mance laughed at himself, and turned back to the screen.

Volk ran his hand over the controls and lengthened the digitized image. "Now?"

Mance nodded his approval, then both turned toward the center of the room to inspect Volk's creation.

Shafus lifted the portable projector off the console. He turned it on and targeted the image so it appeared to be standing next to Shule, who was going through a series of dance-like steps. As he did so, a life-size image of Jesus mirrored his movements exactly.

Mance looked at Volk, clearly pleased with the outcome. "That's it."

Shafus set the portable unit down and turned to Mance as Volk recorded what they had done. "With the projection ready, it's time to finish this."

"Yes," Mance said with some reticence. "I only wish we knew how much was enough."

"We must leave that to Kaseel's better judgment," Shafus counseled. "He's the one that's been closest to this all along." Mance concurred. "If you have the computations ready," Shafus continued, "we could depart as soon as Kaseel returns."

"I'm not sure that's wise," Mance said, shaking his head.

"Liam feels Jesus is out of danger," Shafus reasoned. "He's also had our basic language transfers, though his fluency will be somewhat limited. Still, he should be able to communicate when he awakes."

"I don't want to leave Earth's orbit before he knows," Mance insisted. "We owe it to him to wait. Things will be hard enough for him." Mance looked concerned as he stood up and walked toward the door. He turned back: "Good job all," then left the room.

CHAPTER 5

Several days later Mance and Shafus were moving down one of the ship's corridors on their way to life functions. As the person in charge of the crew's emotional stability, Shafus was concerned by recent silences on Mance's part. They were so unlike him.

Shafus was an unassuming individual; caring, passionate, but very easy to talk with. He was not a psychiatrist or psychologist in the traditional sense. His society's culture and their overall genetic makeup were so well balanced that mental disorders were virtually unheard of. However, as with all enlightened species, there was a quest for new knowledge, and new ways. Even with the demise of his home planet, he still took his job of cataloguing the cognitive processes of various alien species quite seriously. He also kept one eye on the health of the crew, for their present circumstances were extreme, and mild cases of depression were not unusual.

"You were right the other day," Shafus freely admitted, "about staying in orbit. It should have occurred to me."

"Not to worry."

Shafus waited several seconds, expecting more, but nothing came. "You are having doubts?"

Mance did not answer. He just kept moving.

Shafus waited a few more moments, then gently probed further. "What are your concerns?"

Mance's pace slowed, then stopped. He knew he had been struggling, and there was no need for him to face these difficult issues on his own. It was not intended that one person should carry all the burden. He had friends on board who wanted to help, and it was time he sought their counsel. He turned to Shafus, ordering his concerns.

"I've been experiencing some serious misgivings about our involvement, and I'm not sure if they have been brought on by selfishness, or practicality?"

"I assure you, selfishness is not an attribute I would associate with you, Mance. As for your practicality, it is essential to our safety."

"Then I will tell you what they are. We have never used our ability to travel forward in time this way. To affect another culture. It is a serious responsibility."

"It is a serious responsibility to do nothing as well," Shafus countered.

Mance paused to consider, then continued. "I also have this ship and its crew to worry about. It's my priority, and as such, I need to weigh the consequences and ask myself, what will we get from it all? What is the point for this crew?"

Shafus looked at his friend. "If all goes well, satisfaction. Perhaps enlightenment. Maybe even thanks."

"And if all doesn't go well?"

"We are trying to help them, Mance, not hurt them. You've heard Jesus speak. If things don't go well, it will not be the result of something we did, or that Jesus said. It will be brought on by mankind himself."

They continued toward life functions. When they reached the entry, Mance paused and put his hand on Shafus' shoulder. "Thanks, my friend. I should have spoken to you much sooner."

"Let's move forward, Mance. It's really the only direction we have to go."

Mance smiled. He admired Shafus' heart.

The iris-like door opened. Liam and Thelis were already busy making preparations as Mance and Shafus entered.

Mance peered into the stasis chamber. "How soon?"

"Pressure and temperature are normal. We should start to see movement any moment," Thelis responded.

Liam took one final check of the life function displays, then, assured everything was satisfactory, touched a few lights. With a hiss, the chamber's lid broke its seal and began to rise.

"Everything seems stable," Liam said, still monitoring the readouts. Let's hope there was no brain damage.

Very slowly Jesus was coming into consciousness. The first sign was a deepening of the breath, probably a result of the slight difference in air pressure, though he also seemed vaguely aware of a different odor as well. His eyes began to move beneath the lids, but he did not open them right away. Instead his head tilted to the side as his hearing came on line, taking in the foreign sounds of the electronics. It was as if he were already aware of his strange surroundings, afraid to confirm it with his sight.

"Lower the lights to half, Mance."

Mance immediately complied with Shafus' request, running his fingers quickly across the lighting panel. With that Jesus' eyes began to open.

He stared at the ceiling, unable to put these totally unfamiliar surroundings into any, even vaguely, definable context. Though there was nothing remarkable about the fabricated metal from the aliens' point-of-view, it was still more than Jesus could grasp. His eyes continued to focus on it for a few moments, the aliens giving him all the time he needed. Finally, he tilted his head to the side and looked at Shafus.

"Welcome." Shafus smiled.

Thelis moved closer. "May I check your pupil response? Your eyes?" His tone was reassuring and Jesus studied his face without fear as Thelis proceeded with steady ease. When he was finished, Thelis spoke slowly, and deliberately: "I'm going to ask you a few questions. I just want you to nod yes, or no. Do you understand me?"

Jesus nodded yes.

"Do you feel any pain?"

No.

"Good," Thelis continued, "Are you warm enough?"

Yes.

"So you are feeling fairly comfortable?"

Yes.

From the other side, Shafus touched Jesus' arm gently. "Do you feel that?"

Jesus turned toward Shafus and nodded yes.

"And you can see and hear me clearly?" Shafus went on.

Yes.

"No problems then?" Shafus' voice was full of warmth and good humor.

No, Jesus nodded, his eyes still wide with wonderment and confusion. "Excellent!" Thelis exclaimed. "Everything looks good," he whispered quietly to the others.

Jesus fought to open his mouth, his muscles aching from inactivity. His voice was weak, but deliberate, his mind alert, working.

"I understand you, though I know I have never heard these words before. Where is this place?"

"To explain would be impossible at this point," Shafus responded.

"You simply do not have enough information yet. But your health is stable, and it is best that you sleep now."

"But…"

"In time you will come to understand all this."

"Please, be assured that you are safe with us," Thelis offered.

"I have always been safe." Jesus' reply had barely escaped his lips before he fell back into a deep sleep.

"Of course," Thelis said with a smile of admiration.

Liam turned from the displays he had been monitoring and whispered: "he rests."

CHAPTER 6

It was bound to happen sooner or later. The pundits had been talking about the inevitability for years. Ever since the breakup of the former Soviet Union, and the expansion of the nuclear club, it was getting ever easier for terrorists to acquire weapons grade plutonium. Some governments, like North Korea were giving it away. They felt that if the terrorists succeeded in disrupting the western powers, so be it. If not, those powers would still have to expend so much capital in counter measures, it would nonetheless still constitute a kind of moral victory.

The internet and AI had also made their contributions, creating a thermonuclear explosion of information in bomb design and construction, making the horror all the more likely. Still, when the event actually occurred, the world was not only in shock, it was in denial.

Why the terrorists had chosen that particular target was unclear. Perpetually harassed by the IDF it had forfeited its claim to being a hotbed of terrorist activity. The Asian subcontinent was in far more danger presently. But the experts agreed it was only the tip of the iceberg, simply proof these terrorists had the ability, and would stop at nothing. There was little doubt, however, the real quarry was somewhere else, and the stakes had yet to be revealed.

The newsroom was awash with activity as the network rushed to get the special report on the air. Andrew Barr, the news anchor, hurriedly put on his suit coat as a young man powdered his face. A woman strode by and handed him copy which he read as he walked with her toward the news desk. He shook his head, his eyes exuding concern. He looked at the woman whose face reflected his own feelings: "This is one report I'd rather not give."

"Ten seconds till air time." One of the cameramen had his hand raised. "Standby."

Barr sighed and sat in his chair. After a few moments, the red light came on as the cameraman dropped his hand.

"Good evening ladies and gentlemen, this is Andrew Barr with a GBC News, Special Report."

"Just a short time ago, on the other side of the world, something the experts have dreaded for years has come to pass. At 6:15 a.m., Eastern Standard Time, terrorists detonated a small nuclear device within the confines of the city of Beirut. Casualty figures are unavailable since all communication with the city has been broken, but it is feared that fatalities may range into the hundreds of thousands, and likely more..." On the studio monitors clips of the devastation supplanted Barr's image.

"It is not known who planted the bomb," he continued, "but unconfirmed reports indicate several pro-Iranian, Iraqi, and Palestinian terrorist groups have already claimed responsibility, while others in the same groups deny it emphatically. One threat hinted that Jerusalem may be a future target. Nations throughout the world have placed their forces on alert..."

The same day, in a small hotel room, somewhere in the Middle East, four people were watching the same news broadcast. One was a well dressed, middle-aged man in a tailored suit. He was known to the others only as Wick. The remaining three were younger, and far less refined; two males, and one female. All three were casually dressed, and smoked incessantly.

They were terrorists; handpicked, ruthless, each a well educated specialist, and all dedicated to their cause—money. The three had no particular fondness for Wick, but he had proven reliable, and dealt only in cash. And since they had no idea who was supplying him, they learned toleration. It was a perfect symbiotic relationship. They got their money, and Wick stayed alive.

One terrorist, who went by the name of Dace, kept jiggling his foot nervously as the broadcast continued.

"At this time details are sketchy at best, and GBC has been unable to contact any of its Beirut correspondents. It is feared that all may have been killed in the blast. The Red Cross is urgently requesting donations of money, food, blankets, and clothing, and nations around the world are pledging support. The United States hopes to send in supplies and medical teams as soon as their safety can be assured…"

Wick turned down the sound. He looked at his accomplices, and after a moment of silence said, "Well done. They've taken the bait."

"Let the Holy Wars begin," Dace responded, snuffing his cigarette.

"Just make sure phase two is equally successful. There can't be any traces."

"Relax, Wick. It's foolproof," the woman responded brusquely. Her name was Kobra, and though Arabic in origin, its English sounding counterpart seemed extremely fitting.

"It better be," Wick responded, doing little to mask his disdain. He hated dealing with the likes of these.

CHAPTER 7

I am Shafus, the ship's envoy, among other things. I would like to officially welcome you to our little domain."

He unfolded a white robe he brought with him, wrapping Jesus as he sat him up. "The others wanted to be here as well, but it was felt their presence might be a bit overwhelming. They do, however, send their best wishes."

Slowly, Shafus helped Jesus out of the stasis chamber and into the robe, steadying him against the effects of the ship's artificial gravity. Though Jesus was in a weakened condition, it wasn't the field's strength that was the problem, but its weakness. Engineered to provide a modicum of convenience, it did little more then keep things sitting where one left them. The tendency for those not used to the sensation was to overcompensate, rendering their movements a little erratic at first. The adjustment usually didn't take long, but there was always the possibility of bumping into something until it was made.

"Unfortunately, this will have to suffice as your room," Shafus apologized as he glanced around life functions. It had never seemed so austere. "We will, of course, afford you as much privacy as we can."

"This will be fine," Jesus observed, his voice still quite shaky.

Noise from the door sliding open startled Jesus. Mance entered, slowing as soon as he realized what had happened. Jesus studied him for a moment.

"We want you to rest," Shafus continued, "however, feel free to explore should you choose to."

"The crew will answer all your questions," Mance added gently. "All you need do is ask."

"Thank-you." Jesus was feeling his way along. His brain racing on overload.

Shafus pointed to the stasis chamber. "You'll need to get back into this when you want to sleep. It will speed your recuperation. Do you remember how to work it, or do you need a refresher?"

Jesus answered slowly and deliberately. "It's odd. I've never seen such a thing and yet—I know." It was as if he had been given an entirely different brain, which was revealing itself as he spoke. He went slowly, in constant doubt as to whether anything was real. "It is a hibernation chamber, or stasis chamber. Because it can produce variances in temperature and pressure, it is also used as a healing chamber, or hyperbaric chamber. The increased pressure helps speed recovery." He pointed to the side of the unit. "This is the control panel. Am I right?"

"Correct. You're doing very well." Shafus glowed with excitement.

Jesus smiled, beginning to trust and enjoy the experience. "Thank-you." He laughed out loud. "I wish I knew why?"

Mance decided things were well in hand and thought to leave the two alone. "Shafus will stay with you and try to answer your questions. If there is anything I can do to make your stay more pleasant, do not hesitate to ask."

As he began to leave, Jesus spoke. "What do I call you?"

Mance turned. "I'm terribly sorry. I am Mance. The ship's coordinator."

Jesus was momentarily lost in thought. His memory had once again been jarred. "Ship... Yes."

"Yes. Shafus will explain. I'll stop by to see you later." Mance turned and disappeared as the iris closed behind him.

"This is a ship?" Jesus said, turning back to Shafus. He knew, and yet he didn't.

"In a sense. Though of the heavens rather than the water, with which you would be familiar."

"Heavens. Yes. Space travel." Jesus smiled. "I remember now. The Earth is round. Such a strange idea, yet it makes so much sense."

"When you feel up to it, we'll show you, so you can see for yourself."

"I have seen it, even though I know I haven't." A look of dismay shot across his face. "What is happening to me?"

"There is much that is now in your memory waiting for a key to unlock it. As we talk there will be many things you understand without knowing where the information came from."

"Like this language I'm speaking?"

"Yes. So we could communicate more efficiently." Shafus sympathized with the man's quandary. He fought to explain without creating further confusion. "We thought it expedient to use our own language to make the technical facets of the ship more easily understood. Your own language lacked the vocabulary necessary to describe the many…"

"Am I—dead?" Jesus asked in bewilderment.

"You were briefly, but not anymore, I assure you," Shafus replied, smiling. "Aside from needing rest, you're quite alive."

Jesus relaxed only slightly. "I don't understand. I feel like my brain is at war with me."

"You have been receiving information from us electronically; a transfer of knowledge from our computer, directly into your brain."

Jesus' thoughts began racing again as he tapped into another piece of heretofore unknown information. "Computers? Artificial intelligence?"

"That's right. However, the process in your case is far from complete."

"This is possible?"

"Oh yes. Relatively simple really. You see, our computers were designed to emulate our brains. Since both work in similar fashion, the computer simply aligns itself with the different signals and creates a common pattern. The process often works with other species, and we have collected a few similar profiles to yours during our travels. Unencumbered by outside distractions, your brain is able to record information very rapidly…" He could see that he had confused Jesus completely.

"I'm sorry, I don't understand…"

"It is I who should apologize." Shafus bowed humbly.

Jesus studied him for a moment, sensing his embarrassment. "Who are you?" His voice held a touch of innocence and wonder.

"I am—Shafus."

"Yes, I know, but where do you come from? What am I doing here?"

"We are from a place called Kel."

"Kel?"

"It is not possible to explain at this point. Nor does it really matter, since Kel no longer exists."

"What happened?" Jesus persisted.

"To put it simply, we ran out of time." Shafus' voice softened considerably.

"Were you attacked?"

"In a sense. By nature, in the form of a neutron star."

Jesus was in over his head again, only this time it was a situation of his own creation. He smiled at Shafus in bewilderment.

Shafus set whatever feelings of grief he was experiencing aside, and moved forward brightly. "Fortunately, you are not running out of time. And in the future, you will know more. In the meantime…"

"Shafus, what am I doing here? What is this all about?"

This was turning out to be more difficult than Shafus thought it would be.

"Our plan is to move ahead in time. To see if we can find a better—setting—for you."

"How can you move ahead…"

"It's really very complicated," Shafus pleaded gently.

"At least tell me the purpose?"

Shafus could see few options. He chose his words carefully.

"Our thoughts were that there may be a time in your planet's future, when your message could reach everyone. Perhaps it would have more—impact."

"But my mission on Earth is complete." There was a tinge of anger in Jesus' voice, and for good reason.

"Still, there were so many who did not hear."

"That is for our Father to decide."

"I meant no disrespect." Shafus lowered his head.

Jesus paused for a moment, trying desperately to regroup. "I must have time to think, to sort the pieces out for myself."

"Of course." Shafus began to leave, then paused. "We're monitoring this room. If you should need to talk, just call out." He smiled timidly.

"Yes. I will."

"I truly apologize if this has been poor judgement on our part."

"It's just so—unexpected," Jesus stated, still totally overwhelmed.

"We felt your words were important. When our planet died, I'm sure it would have helped our people to have heard them."

"The message has already been given."

"True. But, perhaps it won't hurt to give it again."

Jesus looked down. Shafus thought for a moment, thoroughly comprehending what was going through Jesus' mind.

"Everyone has a right to their own thoughts and feelings. No one should dictate to another." He paused for a moment. "Think on it. We will abide by your wishes."

"And if I choose to go back to the cross?"

"That's the one thing we wouldn't be able to do for you. We only know how to trick time going forward. I'm very sorry." Shafus turned and left the bay. Jesus sat in silence, staring straight ahead.

CHAPTER 8

General Shkolnik, the Israeli commander in charge of operations in South Lebanon, was standing before a huge array of reconnaissance photos supplied him by Israeli Intelligence. He went over every detail of the Beirut bombing, searching for clues as to who was responsible, and what they might expect in the future. It was now morning, and the Israelis had sent several planes and ships into the area to get a closer look at the devastation. Images were also coming in from their satellites, as well as U.S. Intelligence.

The entire city had been rendered uninhabitable by the blast. Heavy smoke was still rising over the ruins, pushed eastward by the breezes coming off the Mediterranean. Only a portion of the city was totally decimated, but between high levels of radiation, and fear, it would be a long time before anyone would be moving back in. This once prosperous and beautiful seaside resort had seen its share of problems over the last fifty years. It had come very close to being fully rebuilt, but was now little more than a smouldering wasteland.

"General?"

Shkolnik turned to find his adjutant, Major Grajek, saluting.

"At ease, Major," the general grumbled as he continued reviewing the photos.

"General, word is that the Russians are vetoing the request for an international force to handle the situation."

Shkolnik turned back to him. "Why, for God's sake?"

"They just don't feel like they have enough verifiable information yet."

"All they need do is turn on any television and they'll get all the verification they need."

"They're afraid to commit until they know who's responsible."

Shkolnik released a sarcastic laugh. "It was never intended that they should know, Major. Look."

He pointed to one of the reconnaissance photos. It was true. The detonation had occurred dead center on the Green Line, the symbolic boundary which separated the Christian and Muslim sectors of the city. It also divided Beirut into east and west, and Shkolnik knew the symbolism was definitely no accident.

"That keeps everyone guessing," he said. "The religious zealots. The political factions. Entire nations." He shook his head in disgust. "Whoever did this will stay hidden in the shadows until they've finished their ugly business. And the Russians are fools if they can't see that."

"Do you think they're implicated?"

"Let's hope not, Major." A battle hardened veteran, Shkolnik was still astonished by how deeply affected he was. No Israeli grew up without an intimate understanding of the world's insanity. The general had been strengthening himself against such eventualities his whole life, and had been sure he could stand up to anything. Yet as he looked at the photos, he was overcome with sadness: "I knew it was always a possibility, but I still can't believe somebody actually did it." His voice wavered. "God save our children."

"They'll survive, sir."

"Life should be about more than survival, Major. I'm so sick of this." The general fought to get his mind focused. "Have they sent any rescue teams in yet?"

"The Lebanese fire and medical units are doing what they can. Jordan has offered assistance, of course, as have we, the U.S., and half the world. But by and large, the area is still much too hot."

"Of course."

"Do you think there's more to come, sir?"

"Don't you?" The major's silence "was an answer in itself. "Keep me posted, Major."

CHAPTER 9

It had been little more than a week since Jesus had been brought on board the ship, yet his recovery was progressing rapidly. He was feeling much stronger, and experiencing little in the way of pain. Much of this was due to the Kel's advanced surgical techniques, drugs, and above all, the hyperbaric properties of the stasis chambers. Nonetheless, the Kels were still astonished by Jesus' recuperative powers.

Jesus was in life functions, staring intently at a computer display screen. Though he still had not completed the full battery of neural transfers, his skills and information levels were already formidable. The aliens made pertinent technical information a transfer priority in the hopes it would facilitate his learning. Using the computer was one such priority. He was now not only computer literate, he was gobbling up information, in part due to his inquisitive nature, in part due to the novelty of it all. It was what the aliens had hoped.

He was presently reading about the history of Kel, but a knock from outside broke his concentration. The iris opened after a few seconds and Mance entered, pleased to see Jesus working at the computer.

"How are you feeling?"

"Much better, thank-you," Jesus said, still distracted by the content on the display.

"You enjoy our technology?"

"I'm not sure. I think I'm—addicted."

"Do you feel up to a tour of the ship?"

Jesus' face glowed with enthusiasm as he contemplated the greater wonders he would find outside the room. "Yes. I would enjoy that very much."

"Follow me."

Mance led Jesus out into the corridor, speaking as they walked. "Our people had been space travelers for thousands of your years. This particular vessel, the Resurrection, was designed explicitly to find other life, or locate another place where we might live."

"Shafus said, you ran out of time."

Mance smiled. "Yes. We discovered our planet had very little of it left before it faced annihilation."

"A—neutron star?" Jesus' voice may have been hesitant, but it was clear that he had been listening, and learning.

"Yes. A massive collision between a neutron star and a black hole was imminent in our sector of the galaxy which we called home. The power that would be released would devastate not only our own solar system, but every known planetary system we had cataloged up to that point. We had to try and find something new, beyond the fringes of projected devastation, where we might plant the seed of a new civilization. That eventuality precipitated the construction of this vessel, and gave it its name."

"Our mission was a race against time from the outset. Habitable planets are not that easy to find. This crew was specially selected. They knew they might never see their loved ones again, but they were all willing to pay the price for the good of the species. In the end, the event occurred much faster than we estimated. With objects so immense it is impossible to predict such cataclysmic events with precision. We went back to find our planet destroyed."

"I'm sorry."

"That's kind of you, but it's long past. By the ship's calendar, thousands of years ago; by the planet's, millions. Our instruments had registered an intense burst of gamma radiation long before we arrived. A warning which—somewhat—prepared us for what we discovered."

Mance's voice betrayed the thousands of years of sadness in his heart, yet he did not dwell on it, and Jesus admired his courage.

"How is it that you are all able to live so long?" Jesus asked, trying to divert Mance's train of thought.

"Most of the time we spend in stasis, to protect ourselves from the extreme forces, and the effects of stellar radiation. Our bodies are frozen in an instant to near absolute zero, and the pattern of our life energies is recorded and stored within the computer, in case anything should go wrong."

Jesus stopped. "By energies do you mean …?" He searched, but found himself unable to explain. "Your language does not have the right word," he said, somewhat surprised.

"What we mean is—the patterns of our individual electrochemical energies, and brain waves."

"The word I search for means—that which separates one man from another. The consciousness that makes each one unique, aside from the purely physical. That part of man which keeps on living, even after the physical body dies."

"The 'soul' you spoke of on Earth?" Mance had switched to Aramaic to find the right word. He remembered Jesus using it in his sermons.

Jesus smiled. He enjoyed hearing his native tongue. "Yes. The divine inspiration that God has given to all men."

"Your idea of God is very new to us. Perhaps long ago, one of our ancestors…"

"That you don't understand is not important. That you are kind and caring is. What you do is just as important as what you believe."

Mance motioned to the door ahead. "Shall we?"

They entered the ship's science lab a moment later. Mance led Jesus over to the control console where he and Volk had worked on the holographic projection. In truth, Mance faced this moment in the tour with the greatest trepidation.

"We've been in orbit above Earth for over a year; resting, gathering samples, refurbishing our ship and supplies. One of our crew, Kaseel, spent much of that time on the surface of your planet."

"I remember the day we met, though I didn't understand at the time."

"He was collecting goods and information. Learning as much about your civilization as he could. Language and customs; the good, and the bad. Then one day he heard you speak. His life hasn't been the same since. Nor have ours."

"So that is how you received my words? Through Kaseel?"

"Partially, but not entirely. You see, Kaseel planted a locating device on you, so we could monitor your whereabouts. It also allowed those of us on the ship to hear for ourselves what you had to say."

Jesus found himself sorting through an odd mixture of feelings. While he had nothing to hide, and saw no particular harm in what Kaseel had done, he still found the idea disturbing on some fundamental level. "Somehow I'm not comfortable with what you're telling me. You were—eavesdropping."

"It seemed harmless under the circumstances."

"But it was an intrusion upon my person."

"I suppose it was inappropriate in some ways…"

"In every way! Don't you see what your interference has done? This is not what I told them would happen. Without proof they'll never believe. All will have been for nothing." He fought to quell his rising resentment. "You simply had no right."

"You don't understand," Mance said, trying to ease Jesus' fears, while justifying the crew's actions. "Nothing has changed. As far as history is concerned, you will have died on the cross."

"But my disciples. I told them I would rise."

"We know." Mance picked up the holographic scanner/projector and aimed the device toward the center of the room.

"This is normally used as a research tool. With it we projected a three-dimensional likeness of you for your disciples, and several others to see."

Mance turned the projector on. Jesus stared at the lifelike image of himself. He circled it slowly.

"Kaseel was the one who ran it on the surface, while Shule provided actual animation from the ship. Kaseel assured us that all who saw it were quite convinced."

Jesus studied the image up close. He tried to touch it, but his hand passed right through." I don't believe it. How could you do this?"

Mance took the blows with humility since they were hardly unexpected. Part of him wished he could undo their actions, while another part felt it was still for the best. Above all, he understood the frustration behind Jesus' continued attack.

"You must be proud of your ingenuity."

"I know this must be difficult for you…"

"Difficult? I was supposed to be with my Father in Heaven."

"You were supposed to be resurrected. In a sense, isn't that what's happened?"

"Not like this!"

"Why not?" Mance suggested, suddenly remembering something Jesus had said. "I thought your Father worked in mysterious ways?"

At those words Jesus tried to push his anger aside, searching for another answer. "You are suggesting that this was meant to be?"

"Most assuredly."

"How can you say that?"

Mance's reply was simple, and undeniable: "Because it's happening." After a moment he added, "Or do you believe that our ship's presence at this time, and in this location, is mere coincidence?"

Somehow the idea had never occurred to Jesus. He studied the alien. The anger he was feeling was genuine, but it was becoming less clear as to whom his wrath should be directed toward. Nor was it clear if he was even entitled to that anger. Had their reasoning in this situation been any less logical than his? There was no doubt that the aliens were trying to help, not harm. Was it fair for him to stand in judgement?

Suddenly he said, "Please, forgive my indignation."

"You have nothing to apologize for." Mance felt a slight bit of vindication, but he still had lingering doubts of his own.

Jesus suddenly felt very alone. He searched deep within himself: "This is the only path I see going forward. It must be the way. But I am so very tired, and I fear the world to come will be far more complicated."

Mance laid a gentle hand upon his shoulder. He was no stranger to loneliness himself. "There's no need to worry about that now."

"Let today's troubles be sufficient for the day, right?" Jesus quipped.

"Yes." Mance smiled. He had heard Jesus say this before, and it was good to know his sense of humor was intact. For the moment, Mance had been forgiven. "Come. Just a few more stops."

"Our living quarters are one deck below," Mance said as they moved back out into the small corridor. "All that pertains to science is on this deck; as for running the ship, the deck above. There's a deck for storage, one for recreation, medical and life functions, which you know. And still others."

They entered another room which was dedicated to only one function, and as such, contained only one item.

"This is a transportation device," Mance said. "It moves our bodies from place to place. In technical parlance, a matter/energy converter."

"Why not just walk?" Jesus asked matter-of-factly.

Mance expanded on the idea, explaining that it was for transportation to locales outside the ship, such as the planet's surface.

"You mean I could go anywhere I wanted?"

"As long as we were within range of your destination. The device does have limits, but it's extremely accurate."

"Is it painful?" Jesus asked.

"No. It's more like a very rejuvenating nap. In fact, it's nicknamed the Lift, not only for what it does, but how it makes us feel. Furthermore, since the computer has a profile of our bodies on record, it eliminates foreign microorganisms. We'll eventually build a profile for you, though it will take some time."

"I'll be going through it?" Somehow the idea was not very appealing.

"You already have," Mance laughed. "That's how you got to the ship to begin with." Jesus looked back at the machine, his eyes wide. "We'll show you how to work it sometime." Mance led him gently toward the door. "We'll go to the living quarters now."

Mance lead Jesus across the corridor and into an elevator which was little more than a circular tube. He spoke out loud, commanding the computer's voice activation system. "Lounge, deck four." The door closed and a slight whoosh was heard as the elevator began to move—a simple device which used the vacuum of space as its source of power.

Mance turned to Jesus. "There is one place I will not take you yet, ostensibly the heartbeat of this ship. However, the control room is really Volk's domain, and he would never forgive me if I denied him the opportunity of showing you all his toys."

"Where is he?" Jesus asked.

"Asleep, in his quarters."

The elevator stopped, and the door slid open, revealing a comfortable space with tables and stools. A computer console, a small counter area, water source, and a few other amenities lined the interior wall. There was no exterior wall as such, only a large viewing port which provided a panoramic look out at the universe.

Jesus moved slowly toward the window. Its slight bubble design created the sensation of stepping out into space. The sight was so breathtaking that when his gaze fell on the exterior of the ship, he momentarily lost his equilibrium. Though not huge to beings like the Kels who had grown up with space travel, the ship's size was more than Jesus could grasp. Free floating as it was, added to his sense of disorientation.

Mance moved to help him away from the window, but Jesus did not want to leave. "No. Please, let me stay." He grabbed the safety rail in front of the window and held on tightly, staring intently at the massive blue ball down below.

"What is that?"

"Your planet. Earth," Mance replied quietly, trying to let Jesus have the moment to himself.

"It is—magnificent."

"Yes."

Shafus, Kaseel, Liam, and Thelis emerged from the hall which contained the crew's private compartments on this same deck. They were talking openly. As soon as they saw Jesus across the room, they moved to welcome him.

"We were wondering where you had gone," Shafus said warmly.

"I kept him to myself for awhile," Mance teased. "We did our best to avoid you. So much for quiet," he said to Jesus, indicating his rabble-rousing friends.

Liam moved Jesus away from Mance and lifted his hair. "I'm surprised you have ears left. Mance usually talks them off with technical gibberish." The aliens were certainly not strangers to mischief.

"Not at all. He has been most informative," Jesus said with a smile, sticking up for his guide.

"Are you getting hungry?" Thelis asked. He knew that Jesus had eaten nothing but synthetics since he had come on board. "Would you like a real meal?"

Mance explained that they had kept some of the provisions Kaseel brought from Earth in their original state, rather than synthesizing them. They felt that eating familiar foods would help Jesus' transition, as well as being easier on his body as it adapted to its new diet.

"You should take the offer," Liam chortled, arguably the alien with the driest sense of humor. "It may be your last chance for real food for a few thousand years."

"Thank-you," Jesus said graciously.

As they spoke Kaseel prepared a simple plate of bread and vegetables. When he was finished he inserted them into a microwave oven.

Jesus was moved by the graciousness of his hosts. He sat down on one of the small stools and noticed they were all standing quietly, staring at him. Shafus signaled to his shipmates once he realized the discomfort they were creating, and encouraged them to sit! with an emphatic nod of his head.

"Will you be eating with me?" Jesus asked Shafus who was now seated just across the table.

"If you can call it eating," Liam quipped from the side. Jesus did not understand.

"We eat only synthetics in space," Thelis explained. "Little pills produced by our food synthesizers, balanced for our individual needs."

"But eating is so pleasurable," Jesus responded, a bit perplexed.

"Pleasurable, but bulky," Liam clarified. "Our synthesizer extracts the basics, and dumps anything with taste." He laughed, knowing full well it was better that way, and safer. After all, he was the one who monitored the crew's nutritional needs.

"In hibernation we require no food at all," Thelis added.

When the microwave oven's timer sounded Kaseel removed the plate. He carried it to the table and presented it to Jesus with a simple bow. "Your dinner, Master."

Jesus looked deep into the alien's eyes, then at his meal. He lowered his head in prayer. "Father, I thank thee for this food, and for the company of these new friends. We are here to serve You, and to do Your bidding. Please help us find our way. Amen."

Jesus looked up, a little uncomfortable. "There is plenty here to share. Trust me, I can make a piece of bread go a long way."

Shafus smiled. "Please. Don't mind us."

"Our synthetics remove any sensation of hunger," Thelis said bleakly.

"Their sensations of hunger!" Liam countered.

Though he did not want to appear rude, Jesus found himself continually distracted by the view out the portal. As he looked on Earth, he could not help thinking of those he left behind; the promises unfulfilled, those things left unfinished. He knew they were not his fault, but he still wrestled with a deep sense of guilt while he searched for a solution.

"How does one travel through time?" he said, turning back to his companions.

"Through the manipulation of certain laws of physics we're able to slow our time down relative to that of others," Mance answered. "In this case it will be Earth, though there will not be a profound shift in the time differential until we near the speed of light."

"I don't understand," Jesus said, shaking his head.

"You would not be the first," Liam remarked, though in truth he was well versed in the concept. "I wouldn't worry about it. It will just make your head hurt."

"But we have not begun?" Jesus probed.

"No," Mance assured him.

"Then the people I knew are still alive?"

"Yes. They are still alive."

"This idea of time travel is so…" Jesus hunted for the appropriate word.

"Odd?" Liam offered caustically.

"Heartbreaking." The room became quiet as Jesus rose and moved toward the portal. "I know people who are suffering, right now. And I feel I should be doing something about it, instead of running away. If you had told me we were traveling through time, and that the people I knew were dead long ago, I don't think I should feel so—guilty."

"There is no reason for you to feel so," Shafus said loyally. "You've taken enough upon your shoulders."

"But the task was left unfinished, and I'm still alive."

"It's all rather confusing, I know," Shafus admitted, hoping to ease his anguish.

Jesus thought for a moment, then looked at Shafus: "Remember what you said? To think on it. That you would abide by my wishes."

"I remember," Shafus said, a bit apprehensively.

"There is something I must do," Jesus said resolutely, his expression fixed. "I must be with my disciples."

"Are you sure?" Shafus asked nervously.

"It is imperative, or all will have been in vain." He turned to Mance. "You said the Lift could take me anywhere, as long as it was within range. Is that right?"

"Yes."

"And my disciples would be in this range?"

"Yes."

"Then I can go?"

"Of course. I half expected it."

"When I have finished my tasks, I will return to the ship, and accompany you to the future."

Mance nodded his approval. Jesus seemed at once relieved and anxious. He turned toward the window and looked down at Earth. "What divine inspiration."

Several moments passed in silence before Kaseel glanced at the plate. The meal was only half eaten.

"You didn't like the food?"

Jesus turned back. "Oh yes, Kaseel. Very much. I'm sorry I'm not more hungry." Suddenly he appeared to lose his balance. Thelis and Mance rushed to support him.

"I think it's time you lie down," Thelis remarked.

"I quite agree," Liam added. "You still need a great deal of rest."

"Come. I'll walk you back," Shafus offered, taking over and leading him toward the elevator. As the door slid open, Jesus stopped and turned to the crew.

"Thank-you." Shafus and Jesus disappeared behind the elevator's door.

Several minutes later they entered life functions. Jesus had been very quiet. He had been pondering his decision to go to the planet's surface, and what he would say when he got there. As Shafus prepared the stasis chamber, Jesus finally spoke.

"Shafus, I should not be alive."

"How so? You sacrificed your life as you were supposed to."

"But you saved me."

Shafus stopped what he was doing and turned to Jesus. His hand gently touched the man's face. "What matters is that you were willing."

"I'm not sure what to tell my disciples. They would never understand about you, or this ship."

"Tell them what you would have said if we had never been here."

"But I'd be lying. I was not resurrected."

"Perhaps not in the way you anticipated. But your heart was not beating when you were brought aboard this ship. By any technical definition, you were dead."

Jesus weighed Shafus' words as the alien removed his robe and helped him into the chamber. It was difficult to know what was right in matters so grey. He resolved to stop thinking about it for the moment.

"I wonder what we will find when we get to the other side of time?" Jesus pondered.

"I'm not sure. Perhaps, if your message does get through, we will find a world basking in peace. Who knows. You may have to relax on a beach somewhere. Retire."

Shafus and Jesus enjoyed the image, but neither really believed it possible. Still, Jesus appreciated the heartening notion. The aliens were so unlike his disciples in some ways, so similar in others. As he thought about it, his mind drifted back to the task before him: what he would find, what he would say, what he would feel. It was strange; for all he had been through, he had never experienced such apprehension.

"You must rest for your trip," Shafus said as he moved to close the chamber lid, then adding: "Everything will turn out as it should."

"I know." Jesus reached out and touched the alien's hand. Shafus smiled, then brought the cover down. As he ran his fingers over the control panel, the stasis chamber hissed as it began to seal and pressurize.

CHAPTER 10

The President was standing behind his desk in the oval office, staring out the window. He had been contemplating how the world had gotten into this mess, and what he could do to extricate it. Life at the top was always lonely, but never quite like this. He was feeling a close kinship to Abraham Lincoln, just prior to the Civil War.

Confusion reigned in both the House and the Senate on how to handle the Beirut situation. The lines that were drawn went well beyond mere partisan bickering. Religious intolerance and racial bigotry were both rearing their ugly heads, and in unprecedented manner. Some were even calling for a doctrine of total isolationism. "Zip up the borders, and be done with it!" was their impassioned plea. The public simply mirrored the confusion.

There was a soft tap at the door. "Come."

The Secretary of State entered and set his briefcase on one of the chairs, crossing to the desk without stopping.

"Good evening, Mr. Secretary," the President said, turning away from the window. "How are you, David?"

"Holding up, Mr. President," he said, unbuttoning his overcoat. He was obviously weary, and a little out of breath.

"What's the word from the U.N.?"

"Chaos. Just like everywhere else. The British are with us, the French aren't sure, the Chinese are entrenched, and the Russians still won't budge. Although to tell you the truth, I don't think the Russians are being devious, they're just scared. With all their Muslims, if this turns into a religious war, all Hell's going to break loose for them."

"I understand their apprehension, David, but we can't let events run themselves. Certainly not in this case. And Hell's fury certainly won't be confined to their corner of the world."

"I agree, Mr. President."

"David, I am going to order a deployment of our troops." The President's voice was somber, but firm. "I have spoken with the Israeli Prime Minister. He is sitting on a veritable powder keg, and convinced we haven't seen the worst of it yet."

"I understand, Mr. President. But if they detonate one and it kills some of our men? What then? Are we prepared for war?"

"We're already at war, David. The world has been attacked. Like a global Pearl Harbor. Only this time, we just don't know specifically who we're fighting. But we sure as hell won't find out sitting here doing nothing, and the time has come to put a stop to this once and for all."

"Yes, Mr. President."

"Let's start working out the details shall we?"

"I'll get right on it."

"Keep me apprised."

The Secretary picked up his briefcase and headed for the door. He stopped just before closing it and called back to the President. "You're right, Ted. And don't worry. Your not alone."

"Thanks, David. I appreciate that. Say your prayers tonight."

The Secretary nodded solemnly, then shut the door behind him. The President picked up the phone. "Get me the Secretary of Defense."

CHAPTER 11

The wisdom behind Mance's decision to remain in Earth orbit until Jesus was ready to depart had proven sound. Apprehensions aside, Jesus was grateful for the opportunity to seek closure with his disciples. He was coming to the conclusion that these strange events were part of the grand scheme, and the road to his Father's side was somewhat longer than he had anticipated. He decided to let his Father's hand work its miracles, and prayed for guidance.

It had now been nearly forty days since the crucifixion. During that period of time Jesus had kept in close contact with the Kels through the locator he carried on his person. This time the audio signal had been turned off to afford him privacy. To get their attention, all he needed to do was walk in a simple circle.

His squeamishness over using the Lift had dissipated long ago, and he returned to the ship on numerous occasions during that period. He relied on the Lift to move him inexplicably from place to place, programing the device himself after receiving a tutorial from Volk. The disciples had no inkling of the technology behind Jesus' appearances, and while Jesus was not totally comfortable with the deception, he knew it was for the best.

As the mission proceeded, Jesus seemed to be more at ease, comfortable with what was transpiring on the planet's surface. The Kels never probed, always supportive and patient. Finally, on a day without warning, Jesus returned to the ship, thanked the Kels for their indulgence, and informed them he was ready to go. Nothing more was said.

It was several hours later when Mance entered the ship's control room and put his hand on Volk's shoulder.

"We're ready to get underway."

"Acceleration factor?" Volk inquired.

"One Earth gravitational unit until we're in stasis, then max to light, point nine-five. We'll deploy three time buoys before departure. I want the whole planet covered."

"Parameters?" Volk asked as he fed the data into the computer.

"Try mass communication plus one-hundred, or two thousand years, whichever comes first. Then have the computers put us back into Earth orbit. Have all the information from the buoys correlated and programmed directly for neural transfer."

"Understood."

Outside the ship there were three brilliant flashes of light as the time buoys ignited on their way into Earth orbit. The ship carried a compliment of these devices, particularly useful in situations where there were extended intervals in a civilization's progression toward technological advancement.

Since the ship's ultimate goal was to find other habitable planets, and to catalog other civilizations, the buoys could be left to monitor a planet's growth. They strictly observed and recorded, and had no defensive capabilities whatsoever. The buoys' cameras were powered by stellar radiation, which allowed the units to keep a visual, if somewhat limited record of changes occurring on the planet's surface over vast stretches of time. If a society made the technological leap to electronics, however, it became possible to keep a fairly comprehensive history in the form of radio waves and images carried in broadcast signals. They had yet to find an advanced society without some form of mass communication.

Often thousands of years passed between deposit and retrieval of the buoys. This would be the first time the aliens would use the buoys for this specific purpose—as alarm clocks.

CHAPTER 12

By the ship's clock the crew had been in stasis only a couple of years, but Earth had aged over two thousand. The time buoys had done their job efficiently, particularly in gathering significant amounts of information over the years that constituted Earth's technological revolution.

The neural transfer of that information would take place during the critical phase between stasis and full consciousness. One did not lay frozen for extended periods of time, come back to life, and just jump back up, fully functional. The process took considerable time, and the computer oversaw the initial portion of the procedure. The thaw itself happened very quickly, but the rest of the transition was extremely gradual.

The computer's first assignment was to implement the medical team's Meltdown, the term the aliens affectionately used to describe the process. Thelis and Liam would get their wake up calls several days before the rest, just as a precaution. As a result, their smiling faces were always the first sight to greet the others when they finally opened their eyes. It had been the source of many jokes. This particular Meltdown would require added vigilance given Jesus' distinctly different metabolism.

Life functions was quiet except for the soft sounds of the monitors. Lighting levels were minimal, and all the stasis chambers were empty and in their vertical positions, with one exception.

Jesus was lying in the lone horizontal chamber. His facial muscles twitched in response to the information which was being transferred with incredible speed. Images flooded his brain in its semiconscious state, held prisoner somewhere between dream and reality. When the images were soothing, it could be a wonderful experience, but when the images were violent, it was Hell, for there was no escaping until the transfer was complete.

The rest of the crew was already up and about, tending to their tasks throughout the ship. Overall, they were physically healthy, but Shafus felt their mental states were marginal at best.

All had been deeply affected by what they had learned of Earth's violent history. Some of the visual images had been horrific; they had never experienced anything so violent. Yet no one spoke of it, instead repressing their feelings, and Shafus was uncertain about how to remedy the situation. He certainly didn't feel like talking either, but he knew it was essential to their healing. Though the transfers took place in the stasis chambers, the events were as emotionally traumatic as reality. For all intents and purposes, they had actually lived the experiences, and the delayed affects were catching up to them.

What exacerbated the problem was the composition of the information, a confused mix of fantasy and reality. In some cases it was hard to know what to take seriously. Fictional entertainments merged with news documentaries, and sorting them out was difficult. And of course, there was the question of why anyone would develop such violent, and often sadistic programs in the first place. Shafus thought of the Romans. He concluded that men had not changed appreciably from their ancient predecessors.

There were images of waste, famine, environmental devastation, pollution. Pictures of poachers and slaughtered animals dovetailed with childrens' programming. War movies overlapped actual war footage, and constant speeches, speeches, speeches. Bombings, burnings, lootings, and beatings. Monks on fire, civil strife, pornography, and genocide. Rush-hour traffic, violent sporting events, emaciated children, city slums. And television commercials. Singing frogs, kids in bottles, monsters eating cities—the aliens were emotionally numb.

Of course there were images of beauty, compassion, and intelligence, as well. Valor, kindness, and sacrifice were not unheard of, but these pockets of goodness occupied only a small percentage of the total information received, and that reality depressed the aliens completely.

CHAPTER 13

Jesus was nearing the end of his transfer, and this fact was of great concern to Shafus having just run the gauntlet himself. He stood by the chamber and watched the man closely, prepared to resolve any major ambiguities. The last phase of the journey had been the most brutal for the crew, and Jesus was now in the midst of this wasteland. His face became increasingly distorted as the succession of images bore down on his brain.

Starving prisoners. Dead children on streets in Asia, Africa, and America. Hitler. Nazis. Neo-Nazis. Holocaust survivors. Death camps. Piles of bodies. Killing fields.

Tears began streaming down Jesus' face as the images kept coming; murder victims, terrorist bombings, sabotaged airplanes, school yard killings. Greed, drugs, slums.

A nuclear explosion! The horror of it seemed to last forever as the huge mushroom climbed ever higher, its shock wave racing through the atmosphere, its earth-quaking rumble growing deeper as the explosion progressed.

Jesus' face writhed with pain, his forehead wrinkled, his head moved violently from side-to-side.

A second nuclear explosion; bigger, closer, more devastating than the first! Suddenly the ship shuddered violently, and Jesus' eyes snapped open. Shafus, after momentarily losing his balance, rushed back to the chamber and immediately popped the lid.

By the time Mance got to the control room Volk was already analyzing the situation. It had been only moments since the incident, but it was already clear that there had been substantial damage. Warning horns were sounding, and lights were flashing everywhere. The ear piercing hiss of air escaping somewhere deep in the ship signaled a major hull rupture. It lasted only seconds as the computer sealed the necessary doors to assure pressurization, but it was long enough to send a shiver through the Coordinator's spine.

Mance had been through his share of space emergencies, but this one was particularly violent, and its cause particularly disturbing since their equipment was specifically designed to avoid such catastrophe. In their situation, structural damage was cause for great concern with their abilities to make adequate repairs so limited.

Mance did his best to keep his voice calm although his heart was racing. Volk was visibly shaken, and Mance did not want to add to his anxiety. "What happened?" he said softly.

Volk was puzzled. The information he had gathered wasn't making sense. "The screens didn't activate. It appears we struck something, or it struck us. There are numerous objects floating around up here."

"Any idea what caused the failure?"

Volk looked back over the data. "None. Apparently the screens switched on after the impact. Diagnostics indicate they are functioning perfectly."

"Perhaps there's something wrong with the diagnostics?" Mance offered.

"Not that I can tell."

"Well, see what you can find. We've got to know what caused the malfunction. What about damage?"

"We have hull damage in the lower left quadrant. Near recreation."

"How bad?"

"Hard to say for sure." Volk checked his data. "Based on the speed of depressurization, I would say it's repairable. Recreation has been sealed off, so we'll have to inspect from the outside. All environmental systems are functioning normally."

"Well, at least that's something."

"It's a good thing no one was in recreation."

Mance nodded. "I'll suit up and take a look."

Volk glanced at the display and called out just has Mance was leaving. "Mance, there's something floating inside the ship's screens." There was a cautionary note in his voice. "Could be what hit us."

Mance stepped back into the control room. Volk worked the console, attempting to get a fix on what they were dealing with. Seconds later Shafus entered.

"That was rude," he joked nervously. "Is everything all right?"

"Our screens are malfunctioning," Mance said, turning to him. "We took a hit, and sustained some hull damage."

"It shook up our passenger pretty badly too," Shafus conceded.

"How is he?"

"Stasis was harder on his body than ours, but his signs all look strong, if a little uneven. I told him I'd come back as soon as I found out what was going on. We couldn't raise you over the intercom."

"Life functions is only one deck from the point of impact," Volk responded as he continued working. "Some of the ship's communications in that section may have been damaged."

Mance could feel himself getting edgy. "I've got to inspect the hull. Maybe it will give us answers about what went wrong. We can't afford to let it happen again." He turned specifically to Shafus. "Keep Volk apprised of Jesus' status so he can pass the information along to me."

"You're going outside to inspect?" Shafus asked Mance uneasily. In his estimation, space suits were far too thin to afford enough protection.

"I have to. Recreation is sealed off."

Shafus grabbed Mance by the arm. "You be careful. Based on what we learned from the time buoys, who knows what's floating around out there."

"I know," Mance responded, indulging his friend's concerns. In truth, he had other things more pressing on his mind.

Suddenly Volk turned to them. "Mance, I think I know why the computer didn't activate the screens. You're not going to believe this." He seemed perturbed by his discovery. "Whatever's out there between us and our screens keeps fading in and out. I would guess that it was specifically designed to avoid detection. Our systems never saw it."

The intricate system of protective screens was a marvel of design. It started with the ship's fusion reactors, which were powered by granules of extremely dense material the aliens had discovered eons before in free space. These granules were believed to be composed of microscopic remnants of neutron stars. Small enough to escape the immense gravitational fields, they were spewed into space during cataclysmic collisions with quasars and black holes. Harnessing the power of their gravitational fields to induce a fusion reaction, the aliens designed a power source capable of sustaining a ship in perpetuity. Thus the computer was free to draw sufficient energy to protect the ship at extremely high velocities, where impact with even the smallest particle could cause catastrophic damage.

The grid itself was composed of powerful, overlapping energy beams which shielded the ship, destroying or deflecting objects long before they ever got close to the hull. If the computer's sensors detected a larger object, it increased the power accordingly. If the object was too large, or too dense to handle, the navigational computers kicked in vectoring the ship around it. At slower velocities, such as when they reentered Earth orbit, the sensors had more time to respond, and the screens only engaged when there was a need. That way, energy could then be diverted to life support, and other essential systems since the crew was no longer in stasis. This distribution of energy on a prioritized basis had proven an extremely effective and energy efficient design, and had the added benefit of allowing for smaller reactors. This was the first time the system had ever let them down.

Mance's thoughts drifted back to the control room when he heard Volk add, "I'm picking up traces of radiation. Whatever is out there, it's very dirty."

Mance reflected on the possible nature of the object sitting inside their screens. If it was avoiding detection, it had been specifically designed to do so. Furthermore, since the time buoys had not collected any information on the existence of this mysterious object over the public airways, it meant that they had been kept secret. As such, he was sure they served no constructive purpose. It was possible that the radiation was coming from a propulsion system, but he wasn't counting on it.

He looked at his two shipmates and saw the concern on their faces. In an effort to break the rising tension, he optimistically blurted out, "I guess we're lucky we only hit one."

Silence. Mance could see they were not amused. He put his hand on Volk's shoulder, "When I go out, don't drop the screens."

Shafus did not like what he was hearing, and Volk was absolutely peppery when he said, "Are you sure that's wise?"

Mance was studying the display, "There's too much floating around up here. I don't want anything else hitting the ship."

"But we're not moving," Volk countered.

"But we don't know if we hit it, or if it hit us?"

"The sensors are showing nothing else in the immediate vicinity." Volk was not giving up.

"But we don't know for sure if the sensors are working properly yet. And even if they are, whether they could detect whatever it is that's out there, or others like it."

Sometimes Volk hated logical arguments.

"I don't like it. It's too dangerous," Shafus stated emphatically, bolstering Volk's position.

Mance turned to him, "I'll be fine, Shafus. Until we know for sure, this is best."

"Stay well away from the screens then," Shafus scolded. "Volk will monitor your position as closely as he can." He glanced at Volk for visual confirmation.

Mance smiled. "I know he will." He turned to Volk: "I'll alert you when I'm ready," then he headed for the cargo bay.

Shafus and Volk exchanged frowns. Each knew what the other was thinking.

By the time Shafus returned to life functions Jesus was already sitting up, his feet dangling over the edge of his chamber. He looked exhausted.

"How are we doing?" Shafus asked, trying not to reveal his concern about what was transpiring elsewhere in the ship.

"I had a nightmare. Horrible dreams." Jesus kept looking at the floor, shaking his head as he grappled with the images now lodged in his memory.

Shafus thought for a moment about lying, or at least softening the truth. But something inside told Shafus that Jesus already knew.

"It was the information collected by the buoys." Shafus offered gently. "We all saw the same things."

Jesus, of course, already understood. To know the future, however, was one thing. To see it, something quite different. "How long have I been asleep?" Jesus asked, still groggy.

Shafus smiled. "About two thousand years. Welcome to your twenty-first century." He helped Jesus to his feet and walked him to a seat.

"Is everything all right with the ship?" The memory of the violent collision had reestablished itself in his consciousness.

"We collided with some space debris as we were entering orbit. Mance is checking it now."

CHAPTER 14

Mance usually enjoyed his space walks. The sensation of freedom was liberating after the tight confines of the ship. The opportunity did not arise often, a tribute to the vessel's design, and a lot of good luck. When they did occur, it was generally the result of a minor malfunction in a unit located on the outer hull. Communications, shielding, and ship's sensors, all had components that were externally mounted.

This trip, however, was very different. While Mance had been very careful to hide his fears inside the ship, privately, his sense of foreboding was acute.

His concern about the damage to the ship was paramount. If the rupture could not be repaired sufficiently for travel at high velocity, they would be stuck in orbit around twenty-first century Earth. It was not an idea he relished, for he was certain that they would never find a home in this society. Humans were still too skittish to accept new things. Especially aliens.

Nor did he feel disposed to die aboard a crippled vessel. He knew it was possible to find the necessary materials on the planet to affect repairs, but advancements in Earth technology, and the immense population, would make it far more difficult for them to do so with anonymity, and the human race's level of fear and distrust, as well as their violent nature, made him shudder to think of how their presence would be accepted should they be detected.

As for the device that had been ensnared by the ship's screens, he was concerned, but reasoned that if it were going to do anything as a result of the impact, it would have done so already. To Mance's way of thinking, it would simply be a matter of dropping the screens long enough to move away from it, then powering the screens back up. But he needed visual confirmation first, and felt confident that his environmental suit was more than capable of protecting him from the radiation for a short period of time.

Mance entered space from the ship's loading bay hatch. His powerpack had enough oxygen for about two hours with moderate exertion, easy enough in the weightless conditions. It also had small thrusters with a ten minute endurance, more than sufficient for propelling himself around the ship, since only short bursts were required. Anything more might send him hurtling out into space. His helmet was equipped with cameras, and he was sure that Volk was watching every move he made.

The first thing he caught sight of as he moved to the point of impact were the pieces of twisted metal surrounding the gash. Though it was certainly nasty, Mance was relieved to find that it was only a couple of meters long, and just a few centimeters wide. The good news was it had breached only one section of the hull, rather than stretching across several. They would be able to repair the damage with the material and equipment they had on board.

"Whatever it was, it took a pretty good bite out of the ship, but I think we can fix it," Mance said as he flashed his light across the length of the damage. He wanted Volk to get a good shot of it on his display. Once the image was recorded they could study it together in the comfort of the ship to determine the best method of effectuating a repair.

"I agree," Volk said as he monitored the transmission. "It won't be simple, but it's doable." By this time Shafus and Jesus had entered the control room. The image on the display began to move upward. Volk responded immediately. "What's happening?"

"I'm going to see if I can locate our mysterious intruder," Mance said as he gave the thrusters another shot. "I don't see anything on this side so I'm going over the top."

"I don't like this, Mance. Not with the screens up."

"I'm well away from the screens," Mance said calmly.

Volk's display showed the side of the ship slowly passing by. Then suddenly the image disappeared as Mance rose over the top of the hull and the sun came into full view.

Mance shielded his eyes. The sun's rays were extremely intense, even with his protective visor down. Because Kel was so much further from its primary star, their eyes were far more light sensitive than human eyes. As his vision began to adjust, the object inside the perimeter of the screens came into view. It was slowly drifting toward the hull.

"I found the culprit," Mance said. He could feel his pulse rate increasing, and fought to keep his breathing steady. He did not want to worry the others needlessly, though he was sure they were probably monitoring his life support systems.

"What is it?" Volk asked, still trying to adjust the camera image to compensate for the intense light.

"I'm not really sure," Mance responded. "I'm going over to take a look."

"Be careful, Mance," Volk warned, each moment getting more frustrated with the equipment and his own desire to see. All they could do was listen, and judge what was going on by changes in Mance's voice.

Mance hit the thrusters lightly. He wanted to keep the ship informed as to what was happening, but he hadn't any idea what the object was. "It is difficult to know what it…." His voice trailed off as he struggled to understand what he was looking at. It's black casing, oddly curved lines, and sharp edges kept him guessing. But as the object slowly revolved its purpose was revealed. "It seems to be… Oh… Oh my…"

"What is it, Mance!"

"It looks like some sort of—missile, or rather missiles. A cluster of them."

"Mance, please! Get out of there," Volk pleaded.

"I'd love to, but that really is not going to solve the problem."

"We can drop the screens and just ease away."

"I'm afraid we don't have enough time for that. Unless you want to leave me here."

"Don't be ridiculous," Shafus scolded.

By this time Mance was close enough to the object to get into its shadow and block the sun. The image finally came up on the display screen in the control room.

"It's getting too close. I've got to try and push it away."

Mance was looking at a multiple reentry vehicle. Part of its cover was torn away, badly damaged by the impact with the ship. It used what Earth scientists referred to as stealth technology, and the ship's sensors were only able to see its signature when the inclination was such that the damaged side of the vehicle was revealed. Where the stealth profile was still intact, the MIRV was completely invisible.

"Don't touch it, Mance." Volk had good cause to be concerned. He knew nothing of the technology, and it was quite possible that it was still very active.

"I can't very well do that, Volk. I've got to move it."

Volk glanced back at Shafus who was doing his best to remain calm. "This is not good," Volk whispered. "I'm surprised it didn't blow itself up, but it still could at any moment." He looked back at the display when he heard Mance.

"It was trapped when the screens snapped on. We're lucky it only hit the ship once."

"Oh yes, we're so lucky," Volk said to himself.

"We're going to have to drop the screens. If this should go off inside the net…"

"Don't even think it," Volk replied, never before believing himself to be superstitious. He ran his hands across the computer panel. "I'm dropping them. Hold your breath."

There was a moment of great suspense as the screens powered down. Volk could not be sure what effect the energy fluctuation would have on the device's electronic circuitry, but there was no other choice.

Floating in space, totally exposed as he was, Mance was thinking exactly the same thoughts. He tried not to focus on it, concentrating instead on the beauty of the world below him. It was still a spectacular sight, even after the intervening two thousand years.

Mance looked up and saw only the remnants of a faint phosphorescent glow as the screens shut down completely. Once Volk confirmed that he was in the clear, Mance gave a short burst from the thrusters and moved toward the object's nose-cone.

As he neared the object he reached out and put his gloves on it very gently. So far so good he thought to himself. He reached over and set the thrust timer on his wrist pad. "I'm go for a sixty second burn."

"That's awfully long. Make sure you leave enough fuel to get back," Volk advised, feeling vaguely parental.

The thruster engaged for several seconds before anything happened. Finally, slowly, agonizingly, it started to move.

"Here we go," Mance called out.

As it gathered speed Mance breathed a sigh of relief, then realized he had never been this far away from the ship in free space. He was starting to feel quite inconsequential. Once the thrusters shut down and he knew he was well beyond the perimeter of the screens, he gave the nose cone one last shove, using the energy to reverse his direction and launch himself back toward the ship. As he moved away from the warhead, he reached down and reset the thrust timer. Then something caught his attention out of the corner of his eye.

The warhead had begun to rotate from the force of his final push. As the open, damaged section of the nose-cone came back into view, Mance could see several lights blinking on and off inside. They had not been doing so before.

"Something just happened. I'm coming back in," Mance stated with some urgency, no longer worrying about his tone of voice. His concern, however, was much more for the ship and its crew than himself.

"What happened?" Volk entreated, unable to see anything since Mance's cameras were not pointed at the warhead.

"I don't know. Lights. Start powering up the screens." Mance's thrusters had shut down. He gave them a long burst manually. Too long!

Volk could see a dangerous situation developing, but he knew it was essential that he try and remain calm. Mance's life might depend on it.

"Don't panic, Mance," he said in the most reassuring voice he could manage. "You don't want to overshoot. I'll wait till your within the net."

"No, now! I should be able to get through before they build up too much strength."

"But…"

"Don't wait, Volk! If this blows up without the screens there won't be any ship!"

Volk had never heard Mance sound so frantic. He ran his fingers across the panel as Shafus and Jesus watched the display holding their breath. The ship's screens' phosphorescent glow was returning just as Mance cleared the perimeter with only a fraction of a second to spare.

Volk breathed a sigh of relief, but it was short-lived. A white hot image suddenly burned across the display screen. A fraction of a second later the ship pitched violently and began rotating out of control.

The explosion disrupted the artificial gravity field and the ship's occupants were sent tumbling in weightlessness, or bouncing into walls where they were held by the extreme rotation generated by the explosion. Slowly the computer regained control, stabilizing the ship with directional thrusters. The crew settled to the floor as the artificial gravity returned.

Though he was inside the screens' protective net, Mance had been pummeled by the effects of the explosion, like a bug caught inside a glass jar that was being brutally shaken. Initially his body slammed up against the hull, then glanced off and flew straight at the screens. There had been several impacts, ending only after the ship's rotation had been brought under control. Each hit had stopped his body violently in a brilliant flash of light, his spacesuit affording only the smallest amount of protection against the power of the screens. When the ordeal was over, he hung motionless in space.

Volk was frantic as he tried to figure out what was happening. The cameras on Mance's helmet were no longer functioning, and he could not tell if Mance was dead, or whether his equipment had simply failed. He was hoping for the best, but his intuition was telling him otherwise.

"Mance!" he called blindly, but their was no answer. Shafus and Jesus were standing at Volk's side, waiting for a response that never came.

Volk called out over the ship's intercom, not sure if that was even working. "Kaseel, get your suit on as fast as you can! Respond if you heard this."

"I'm on my way!" came the reassuring answer.

Shafus put his hand on Volk's shoulder, "I'm going down to the loading bay to see if I can help."

Jesus grabbed Shafus' arm. "I want to come with you."

"Of course." Shafus called back to Volk on their way out: "Volk, tell Liam and Thelis to meet us there."

"Right away. Let me know when Kaseel is ready so I can drop the screens." Volk was already blaming himself. He didn't want to be responsible for two accidents in one day.

Kaseel hit the thruster control and shot over toward Mance. The way Kaseel handled the powerpack was always a bit disconcerting for Volk. As far as he was concerned Kaseel went far too fast. But he had to admit that his young friend worked the thrusters deftly, as though he was born with powerpack attached. On this particular day, Volk had no complaints.

Kaseel got to Mance quickly and saw little sign of life. He grabbed hold of Mance's arm, then maneuvered the two of them back to the hatch which lead to the loading bay. He activated the hatch control on the side of the ship, and the hatch door opened, not nearly quickly enough to suit Kaseel.

Once the bay door was open Kaseel pulled Mance inside the pressurization chamber. Again he activated the controls, now waiting for the door to seal. It seemed like an eternity.

By this time Shafus and Jesus had entered the loading bay and were peering through the pressure chamber window. Kaseel looked up and saw them. He smiled helplessly as he held Mance's limp body in his arms. When the smile left, his face was grim.

When the pressurization was complete the door opened and Shafus and Jesus rushed into the chamber to help Kaseel whose motion was limited by the bulky spacesuit. The three of them carried Mance into the loading bay itself and quickly began to remove Mance's helmet which was totally scorched on one side. Thelis and Liam were set up and waiting.

"Will somebody tell us what happened?" Thelis inquired as he and Liam began to work. "It would help immensely." The others moved aside, their jobs done for the moment.

"The nose-cone exploded," Shafus explained.

"It threw him against the screens," Kaseel added, knowing full well they would understand the implication.

Liam chose not to comment. It was best to keep his thoughts clear at this time. "Let's get him out of this suit. Thelis, check his life signs."

"Is he all right?" a voice called out over the intercom. Volk was still in the control room, running diagnostics and tallying the damage.

"We don't know yet, Volk," Liam answered. "We are taking off his suit right now. Thelis is checking him."

Shafus could see the dismay on everyones' faces. He searched for some ray of hope.

"Volk had armed the screens just seconds before this happened, so they weren't quite at full power yet."

"If they had been, Mance would have disintegrated instantly," Liam noted. "At least they kept him from blowing out into space."

It wasn't the positive reassurance Shafus was hoping for, but at the moment he would accept whatever morsel of optimism he could find. As he reached in and helped Liam remove the remainder of Mance's suit, he noticed Jesus watching from a corner of the loading bay, his face soft and serene, in contrast to the situation's urgency.

The sight of Mance's frail body moved Jesus greatly. These gentle beings had risked much for him, motivated by nothing but compassion for a world that would probably have scorned, or killed them. However, while their bodies appeared frail, their inner strength was truly remarkable, and in that moment Jesus realized just how much he had come to love and admire them.

"The pulse is very weak," Thelis said urgently. Mance had yet to move but for the slight rise and fall of his chest.

"We're too limited here!" Liam looked up at Thelis. "We have got to get him to life functions!"

"I'll carry him," Jesus said stepping forward.

Shafus turned to him. "Follow us."

Minutes later Jesus laid Mance in a stasis chamber, then stepped back so Thelis and Liam could do their job. He looked over at Shafus.

"Will they be able to help him?"

"It will depend on the injuries. The screens are very powerful."

The two doctors worked frantically, trying everything that their training and experience had taught them. After several anxious moments, however, reality set in and they stopped. Thelis leaned over and listened to Mance's chest with one of his instruments. He finally stood up and looked at the others.

"The heart beat is weak, but stable."

Jesus wanted to breath a sigh of relief, but Liam, who was scanning Mance's head with another sensor interrupted: "But brain wave activity has stopped."

No one said a thing for several seconds. Liam was the first to break the silence in an effort to console his friends: "Even at the lowest power settings the screens have enormous strength. It would be foolish to think that such an accident would not result in severe injury and brain damage."

Shafus looked at the others, and added, "We did everything we could." There were a few more seconds of silence, then Kaseel said, "After all this time, it's hard to imagine the ship without him."

"I'll remove the life supports," Thelis said, his hand visibly shaking.

"I don't understand?"

Jesus' voice startled the crew, for he had been standing quietly in the shadows.

Shafus turned to him and explained. "After Mance's body has expired, we will jettison it into space."

"But he's still alive. Where there's life, there's hope."

"Hope is fruitless now," Shafus said kindly. "Some aspects of his body are functioning, but the extremely high power has destroyed his nervous system. His brain is dead."

"It is our custom in such circumstances to remove life support, and let nature take its course," Thelis explained, trying not to upset Jesus further.

"Without life support, I would estimate a day, two at the most." Liam went on about his business, trying to hide his real feelings.

Jesus touched Shafus gently on the shoulder. "Before you move him, would you mind if we spent some time alone?"

Shafus looked at his crew mates. "I don't think anyone here would have any objections."

"I would like to pray for him. It is customary."

"Of course," Liam said. He signaled to the others to clear the room.

The iris on the entryway shut and the room was quiet. Jesus moved toward the stasis chamber which held Mance's body, studying the alien's face. He put his hand on Mance's forehead, then slowly knelt and began to pray.

CHAPTER 15

The crew had assembled in the lounge to determine who would function as the ship's new coordinator. Shafus was talking to Volk over by the viewing portal. Beyond that, few words were exchanged as the crew attempted to put what had happened into perspective. Shafus finally moved to the front of the room to act as interim chairman.

"I just informed Volk of the situation. I know each of you will pay tribute in your own way." After a brief moment of silence, Shafus continued. "No one would have pushed harder to take care of the restructuring of duties under these unique and trying circumstances than Mance. And so it is incumbent upon us to name a new coordinator as quickly as possible."

"I think that choice is clear," Liam declared, looking directly at Volk.

"I quite agree," Thelis added. "Volk knows more about the ship's operations than the rest of us combined."

Volk just stood there shaking his head. When he finally did speak, his voice was full of self-recrimination.

"I saw it coming. I knew it, but I didn't stop him. I have no business being coordinator."

There was a moment of silence. No one agreed with Volk's assessment of the situation, but how were they to respond. It was clear that Volk had taken Mance's death very personally, and it was crucial that the situation be handled delicately so Volk would not carry this burden for the rest of his life. The entire crew inadvertently looked to Shafus.

"You are no more responsible for what happened to Mance than the rest of us," Shafus said while the others nodded in agreement. "Mance did what he felt he had to do, what he would expect any of us to do in similar circumstances. He knew the risks, and would not want you to shoulder the responsibility." He forced Volk to look him in the eye. "You know this to be true."

An odd look of relief and anguish spilled across Volk's face, and a tear rolled out of his eye. Shafus put his hand on Volk's shoulder as he continued, speaking to everyone now.

"It is a difficult time for this to happen. It will be a tremendous undertaking for Volk, especially being short one crew member. However, Shule knows how to run most everything, and I think he has been an apprentice long enough." The comment brought smiles, momentarily breaking the gloom.

Shafus turned to Volk, "Well, it seems to be unanimous."

I will do my best," Volk said quietly, his usual edge now gone with his grief. "I know I can count on everyone's cooperation." He fought back his feelings, and delivered his first directive. "Our number one priority is—determine what is needed to repair the hull. To that end I have moved the ship into a higher orbit to avoid detection and the possibility of another collision."

The whoosh of the elevator's vacuum drive caught the crew by surprise, causing several of them to jump. "That scared me," Shule whispered to Thelis.

"I forgot that anyone else was in the ship," Thelis responded, referring to Jesus.

At that moment the elevator door opened. There was an audible gasp as everything stopped, and Mance stepped forward into the room.

"That was a very close call, wouldn't you say?"

Liam looked at Mance in total shock. His mouth hung open for several seconds before anything finally came out. "Mance... We thought..."

Mance smiled. "You're not disappointed, are you?" His voice was innocent, and happy.

"No," Liam said. "Of course not!" finally letting his joy take hold of him. "It's good to see you, Mance!" though he still wasn't sure he believed what he was seeing.

The aliens all moved in, touching Mance, rubbing his head, hugging him as much to welcome him back as to convince themselves that their senses were still functioning properly.

Something was clearly bothering Thelis, more than mere concern for his patient's recovery. "Are you sure you should be up and walking around already?" Thelis asked, studying Mance's face and head.

"I feel good actually," Mance responded warmly. "I woke up with a start and found Jesus sitting next to me." Mance smiled at Jesus who had been standing near the elevator door. "The last thing I remembered is telling Volk to get the screens back up."

"Yes, and then that thing blew up and hurled you into the ship and the screens," Kaseel spelled out, feeling a bit of disbelief himself.

Even Mance looked perplexed after hearing this.

"Well," he said thoughtfully, "now I understand why you're shocked to see me."

"The screens weren't at full power yet, but…" Volk's voice was a bit shaky.

"Yes, but all-in-all I would have to say I was very fortunate," Mance agreed. He smiled at the others, making no more of it than a lucky break.

Liam put his hand on Mance's shoulder. "As lucky as you are, I still don't think it will hurt for you to rest a little while. Thelis and I feel we should run some tests, just to make sure that everything is functioning as it should." Thelis looked at Mance and smiled in agreement.

"Of course," Mance said without argument.

Liam turned to Shafus and said rather mysteriously, "After we get these tests done, I should like to go over the results with you, just to make sure we haven't missed anything." He speech was very emphatic.

Shafus was puzzled but had no objections. "Certainly. I'll be in the control room with Volk."

With that Thelis and Liam lead Mance into the elevator. Shafus and Volk remained behind, waiting for the elevator to return and take them to the control room. The others had already dispersed into their living quarters on the same deck. Jesus had quietly seated himself at a table near the viewing portal. While he waited, Shafus moved to him and sat on the opposite side of the table.

"Would you care to join us in the control room? Now that Volk has his regular job back he probably has time to familiarize you with more of the equipment."

Jesus looked at him and smiled appreciatively. He looked very tired. "I would like to, but all the excitement has worn me out. Perhaps in a little while."

Shafus touched his hand. "Whenever you like. You're always welcome. Feel free to rest. And thank you for your help and concern."

"There is no need to thank me, but you are welcome just the same." He smiled, then looked away from Shafus, back out at the stars.

CHAPTER 16

The truck had been parked inside the abandoned warehouse near the center of Jerusalem just hours before the door on the side of the building burst open. Sunlight poured in, along with the three terrorists, all toting Uzis tucked from sight, only the silencers on the tips of their muzzles showing. They quickly checked the old building to make sure they were alone.

Basel, the youngest of the three stood guard at the entrance. Weapons were his specialty, and he always welcomed any opportunity to try one out. Dace and Kobra moved to the truck and opened the combination lock on the door. It slid noisily open to reveal a specially outfitted compartment, complete with shielding, bomb, and everything necessary to trigger it. Dace pulled a small infrared remote from his pocket and pointed it at the weapon. He pushed several buttons on the keypad, disabling the intruder sensing system. The numeric displays on the bomb's two timers blinked twice, then remained lit. Dace and Kobra jumped into the truck and proceeded to program the device for detonation.

CHAPTER 17

Shafus and Volk sat at the control room computer console watching one of the display screens, monitoring various Earth radio and television broadcasts. While both had experienced indescribable euphoria over Mance's recovery, a new terror was being thrust at the world, something so potentially devastating that it overshadowed their joy almost completely. Things had deteriorated quickly since the unidentified terrorists had made the announcement. Even the broadcasters, who never seemed to show anything but detachment, were visibly shaken and distraught.

Volk was hard at work, using some of the ship's more specialized sensing equipment to look for any signs of radiation, in, or around Jerusalem. If there really was a bomb, and it was unshielded, or emitting radiation of any sort, they just might be able to locate it before it exploded. It flashed across his mind that these same sensors might have detected the presence of the MIRV long before they had hit it, saving them a lot of agony. He let it go. In retrospect, hindsight was always perfect. But he vowed that he would not make the same mistake twice.

The control room door opened and Thelis and Liam entered looking very resolute. They just stood there waiting. They appeared to be feeling extremely confrontational.

Shafus could feel their moods without even looking at them. Finally he turned to Liam and tried to deflect the onslaught with a smile. "Are you finished with your evaluation?"

"Yes," Liam responded coolly. "We gave him a thorough going over using our most sophisticated equipment and found nothing unusual."

"Nothing!" Thelis added with extra emphasis.

"That's excellent!" Shafus said, turning back to the console. He had a feeling they weren't finished with him yet.

"If you say so," Liam said rather pointedly.

Shafus turned back, confused by their attitudes. He thought for a moment. "I agree that after what Mance went through, that wouldn't seem possible. But since it is, I suppose we should be rejoicing instead of sounding so dour." He looked at the doctors, scolding them with his eyes.

"We quite agree," Liam said, softening his approach, but holding his ground.

"Do you have any explanations at this point?" Shafus inquired.

"Nothing of a scientific nature." Thelis' voice had risen sharply. He was obviously hinting at something.

"Well… I suppose we'll just have to attribute it to luck then." As far as Shafus was concerned the case was closed.

"There was no luck involved here," Liam shot back, unwilling to let the matter go. "There can be only one explanation."

Shafus looked at the two doctors, still not grasping their meaning.

"A miracle." Thelis' voice was assured, without a hint of doubt.

Shafus looked at Thelis and smiled, trying his best to dismiss the idea without giving offense. "Thelis…"

"Shafus, Thelis is absolutely right," Liam said, defending his fellow doctor. "The helmet on Mance's spacesuit was cracked in several places from the impacts!"

"Let's be honest, it was destroyed!" Thelis threw in uncomfortably.

"There was enough power in those screens to protect this ship from a nuclear explosion, Shafus!" Liam exclaimed. "This is no simple matter of luck!"

"It is not as though all our instruments could have been in error," Thelis added, rather indignantly. "The data confirms that what has happened is—impossible!"

"Jesus?" Shafus was being very cautious.

"What other explanation is there?" Thelis implored.

"It goes against my better judgement." Shafus spoke slowly, uncertain as to why the idea was causing him to feel so uneasy. "I have seen many amazing things in my life, to which there have always been logical explanations." He thought for a few seconds. "I would like to speak with him directly."

No one spoke or moved for several seconds, then Shafus left the control room. Liam and Thelis looked at Volk. He had overheard the entire conversation.

CHAPTER 18

Andrew Barr was seated behind the anchor's desk, going over the copy. It was a job he had always relished. He had certainly paid his dues, and fought hard to get it. But today he could not help wish someone else were occupying his seat. The news was terrible, the consequences horrifying, and it was next to impossible to keep his emotions at bay. When the red light on the camera flashed on, and the cameraman dropped his hand, he gathered himself together.

"Ladies and Gentleman, GBC News has just learned more about the ultimatum given to the Israeli government concerning this second round of nuclear extortion. We go live to the outskirts of Jerusalem and GBC field correspondent, David Hiller."

Barr's image was replaced by that of a man dressed in khakis. David Hiller, a handsomely rugged man in his mid-thirties, was one of those journalists who had no other life outside of the story he was covering. War was nothing new to Hiller, in fact one sensed that he was at home in this element. He stood with microphone in hand on a dusty hilltop, and some distance away, the ancient city of Jerusalem formed his backdrop.

"David, what can you tell us about the ultimatum at this time?" Barr probed from the studio.

"There is not much to tell, Andrew," Hiller said, looking straight into the camera. "In fact, I don't think ultimatum is the right word. It was a flat-out warning that the city would be destroyed, and that there was only one hour left to evacuate."

"Was any reason given?" Barr questioned, a bit of irony seeping into his voice.

"Yes. It was stated directly. If they can't have their Holy City, no one will."

"Who are they?" Barr continued. "The Palestinians?"

"They did not identify themselves, Andrew. It could be Hezbollah, Hamas, Shiite Fundamentalists; throw in a few Christian and Jewish sects to boot. The fact is, it would be pointless to jump to conclusions, with one exception—it has to be someone, or some organization, with a lot of money."

Hiller knew that the technical information was now within the public domain, but the fact was that actually building a bomb; getting the materials, transporting it, planting it, hiding it, was still an incredibly expensive proposition.

"Are the Israelis certain this threat is for real?" Barr supposed the audience would feel the question was terribly callous, but it was an important issue and he asked in earnest. Fortunately, Hiller's response validated his rationale.

"That's a problem, Andrew. On the one hand you've got to take every threat seriously given what transpired in Beirut. But on the other, you don't want to jump every time someone says boo! You'd waste too much energy. However, in this case, that's not a problem because we know for sure. The bombers referred to some weapons grade plutonium that disappeared about a year ago from Pakistan. A theft that was never made public. The Israelis received a detailed description of the incident which left little doubt: These are the people who took it, and this threat is for real."

"Is there any way to negotiate with them?" Barr asked.

"These people don't want to negotiate, Andrew. They want to create chaos, and on that score, they are doing very well. What's more, it would appear they have enough plutonium for several more bombs."

CHAPTER 19

The door to the life functions lab slid open and Shafus poked his head in. A Mozart symphony was playing, and Jesus sat listening, enjoying the novelty, as well as the beauty of it. Thanks to the time buoys, a library of Earth's music now filled their data banks.

"Am I disturbing you?" Shafus said over the symphony.

"No," Jesus replied, immediately turning down the volume.

"I knocked several times but…" Shafus stopped to listen. Unlike Jesus, he was familiar with recorded music. His people had a rich musical heritage. But this was unlike anything he had ever heard before. He sat beside Jesus and closed his eyes, enjoying the delicacy, and the richness.

After a few seconds Jesus spoke, his voice apologetic. "I stopped listening to the news."

"You heard about what's going on then?" Shafus said without opening his eyes.

"Yes."

"Well, I don't blame you."

"I needed to think," Jesus explained. "Things are happening so fast down there."

"Good thinking music." Shafus smiled and kept listening.

"I have never heard anything so glorious," Jesus said with admiration. "This Mozart was truly a gifted man."

"Yes." Shafus paused, then added, "Like you."

The comment had been deliberate and Jesus looked at Shafus, suddenly feeling caught off guard. "To what are you referring?"

"I'm referring to Mance's recovery," Shafus answered, working the conversation like a game of chess.

"What of it?" Jesus said turning away.

"Rather astounding, don't you think?" Shafus looked directly at him, all pretense now gone from his voice.

Jesus shrugged. "Astounding things happen on occasion."

"But there is always an explanation."

"Perhaps you should think of it as—a gift from life."

"Is that your explanation?"

"I have one that works for me," Jesus said simply. "I am not sure that you would be satisfied."

"Does it involve your God?"

"He is your God too, Shafus." There was a moment of silence. "As I said, I did not think you would be satisfied."

"I regret appearing so skeptical," Shafus apologized. "After all, these are some of the very reasons we brought you here. However, to hear about miracles is one thing; to experience one first hand…"

"Why are you so certain this was a miracle?" Jesus probed.

"Our instruments tell us that what happened to Mance was beyond repair by any known technology."

"Instruments can be wrong," Jesus replied. "Perhaps there are greater technologies than you are aware of. Call it faith. Faith in a power that is bigger than we are."

"Collective strength?" Shafus remarked, unconvinced.

"Perhaps. What it's called is unimportant."

"No matter what definition we settle on, the facts are unavoidable. Without you, Mance would not be alive. Of that we are sure. For that, we thank you. "

"It is not me you should be thanking."

Shafus smiled. "Lacking your 'faith' as you put it, we prefer the concrete, that which we can see and feel."

"Isn't Mance something you can see and feel?"

Shafus' forehead wrinkled. His own logic had been cleverly trapped. "You give me a great deal to think about." He smiled, then after a moment, stood to go.

"Shafus? Is there anything we can do?"

"You mean about Jerusalem?"

"Yes."

"I don't know. Volk is using all the ship's resources to try and locate the device right now. What we do if we find it, will depend on where, and when, we find it. In truth, this ship is not equipped to deal with conflict of that sort."

"Things seem so out of control."

Shafus raised his brow. "Yes. I guess we will have to have—faith."

Jesus looked at him and smiled.

Shafus stood at the door another moment and listened to the recording. "Exquisite music." He shook his head as he searched for words to express his feelings. "Man is such an—enigma. Such beauty. Such horror." He looked at his friend. "I have much to do."

Jesus called after him as he was leaving. "God be with you."

Shafus stopped and looked at him for a moment. A grin spread across his face. Then he turned and left.

CHAPTER 20

All roads from Jerusalem were in total chaos. Cars and trucks were engulfed by masses of people fleeing on foot. Scores of vehicles had been abandoned once the owners realized that saving their property was not only hopeless, it was actually hindering their chance to survive. The stranded vehicles, however, ended up making a bad situation even worse.

A military Humvee was pulled off to the side of the Hebron Road, and two Israeli soldiers watched the progress of the evacuees. There wasn't much they could do if trouble broke out, but they were there to help if they could. For the most part people behaved themselves, their only ambition being, to get as far away from the city as possible.

The heat from the sun was so intense that the procession took on a surreal quality as one of the soldiers, a young lieutenant named Reiss, peered through a set of binoculars. What he saw dismayed him, for the line of people stretched beyond the railway station, nearly all the way back to the walls of the ancient city, and time was quickly running out.

CHAPTER 21

The control room was quiet for the moment, which was often not the case. As the heart of the ship, the control room often received an immense amount of traffic, and it was not unusual for Volk to keep the door secured in the open position, to cut down on the noise created by sliding metal and pressure seals. Such was the case today.

Mance sat at one end of the ship's vast control console, Volk at the other. They were wearing headsets and switching from broadcast to broadcast in an effort to collect as much information as they could. Shafus entered without them knowing and tapped Volk on the shoulder.

"Any luck?"

Startled, Volk pulled off his headset, but kept working as he talked. "Nothing yet." He paused, then added sadly, "They don't think they can evacuate everyone in time."

"Their one hour deadline was given almost forty-five minutes ago," a voice said from behind.

Shafus turned and saw Mance removing his headset. "Why won't they wait until everyone's left?" Shafus asked.

"Who knows," Volk responded grimly. As far as he could tell, the point, if there was one, seemed to be to take some lives, but not all. That many of the lives you did take were innocent, was totally immaterial. It was all very convoluted, and he was sure he would make a lousy terrorist. In fact, at the moment, he was wishing he had never heard of Earth.

"What do they desire in return for stopping it?" Shafus queried, still trying to make sense of the situation.

"Nothing. They won't stop it," Mance stated matter-of-factly.

"Why would somebody blow up a city for nothing? What would be the point?"

"A commentator said he thought it might be a business cartel," Mance explained.

"A what?" Shafus vaguely remembered the term from the transfers, but couldn't place its meaning.

"In this case, a coalition of arms dealers. They sell weapons; guns, tanks, bombs, missiles…

"Jerusalem is their world's holiest city," Volk went on. "Three religions claim it as their own. It seems a Holy War could be very profitable."

Shafus could not believe what he was hearing. "Surely the religious leaders wouldn't buy into that?"

"An interesting choice of words," Mance noted, unconvinced. He paused. "Any thoughts on how to proceed here?"

"You're referring to Jesus?" Volk inquired.

Shafus was shaking his head nervously. "The question I keep asking is should we proceed?"

"Why?" Mance asked him.

Shafus thought for a second. "When we started out, I was certain we were doing the right thing. Now I'm not so sure."

"I think that with the best of intentions we've created a situation for which there is no good solution," Volk said sadly. His statement was so simple. And so true.

"We're not involved yet!" Shafus stated emphatically. "He doesn't have to go. If we send Jesus down there his life will be in peril, and I have no desire to send him to his second death."

"We knew that was a possibility from the start," Mance reminded him.

"Not like this!" Shafus shot back sharply. His anger, though modulated, was very out of character. "We brought him here to give him the chance to communicate something wonderful, not deliver him into the throes of insanity!"

"Is it anymore insane than what he came from? I think we need to let him make that decision," Mance said, trying to calm Shafus. "'If all goes well?' Remember that conversation?"

"I take it back." Shafus slumped into one of the seats, exhausted by his own frustration. "Killing makes everything so complicated."

"I want to go."

Shafus turned and saw Jesus standing near the open door.

"It must be done. The time to act is now." His voice was calm, and he seemed to have clear purpose of mind.

Mance rose and moved toward him. "Do you have any ideas about what you would do?"

"No. But one thing is certain, I will accomplish nothing here in the safety of the ship."

"Where would you go?" Mance asked, hoping for something a little more substantial.

"To the heart of the matter. Jerusalem."

Shafus was feeling helpless. "What do you hope to accomplish there? If they do set off a bomb, you'll be killed."

Jesus looked at him and smiled. "Jerusalem has always been a difficult place for me."

"That's not funny," Shafus said, moving away.

Jesus stopped him. "Something made you bring me here. Have faith in that. Don't be afraid. I'm not."

"Isn't there something else you could do, someone else you could talk to?" Mance asked. "A government leader?"

"Yes!" Shafus perked up, seeing some daylight. "They know of you. And they invoke God's name all the time. I've heard them."

"You do not understand the skeptical nature of human beings. They would not recognize me, even if I told them." Jesus knew that identifying himself publicly would spell disaster. He would no doubt be labeled a lunatic. Besides, the world's governments seemed totally immobilized by the situation.

"Then religious leaders," Shafus suggested, searching for anything.

"There are so many. Who would I see? The others would denounce me because I had not spoken with them, after all, many are little more than politicians themselves." Jesus looked at each one of them. "Jerusalem. My destiny is still in Jerusalem."

"We didn't bring you here to die!" Shafus pleaded.

"I have to die sometime. If this is God's will…"

The room was silent.

"I will go and prepare myself." Jesus started to turn, then hesitated. "I feel the sadness in your hearts. You have become involved in a situation which will undoubtedly bring you pain no matter what you do. There is, much hatred here, and the closer you get to it, the harder objectivity is to come by. But always remember this—I thank-you for what you've done. It was the right thing to do. I see that now."

After he left the room Mance turned to Shafus. "Have Kaseel prepare a locator for him so we can monitor his movements. At least we can try to help him should he…"

"It's time," Volk said, listening over the headset.

"What?" At first Mance didn't realize what Volk was referring to.

Volk listened intently for a moment, then spoke quietly. "The deadline. Detonation should be any second." His hands continued working, even as he listened and spoke.

"Mance, we can't let him go down there. Not now," Shafus entreated.

"Mance! I've got something!" Volk was motioning him toward the display screen. "I think I may have found it! The bomb! There's a very faint, but distinctive radioactive signature in the middle of the city."

"It's not detonated yet?" Mance said, rushing back to the computer console.

"No."

Mance turned to Shafus. "Tell Jesus to wait. Tell him that we may have found…"

"Mance, the Lift was just activated!" Volk's voice was panicky.

"By whom!"

"I don't know. By the time I realized what was happening they were gone."

"Jesus?" The thought had set Shafus' heart racing.

"It had to be," Volk said, trying to confirm it.

Mance laid a calming hand on Volk's shoulder. "Do we know where he went?"

"Why did I ever teach him how to use it!" Volk cried out. He looked at Mance." He's in Jerusalem. I'm sorry, Mance. I had the bomb's location showing on the computer displays."

"It's not your fault, Volk," Shafus said in an effort to relieve his anguish. "It's what he wanted. You couldn't have stopped him." Shafus knew that was true.

"Can you bring him back?" Mance asked.

"He's on the surface already."

"He has a locator."

Resignation spread across Volk's face. "He never got it."

Mance's mind was racing. The ship had plenty of power. There had to be options. "Can you get the Lift to isolate just the bomb?"

"We couldn't possibly move it. The bomb's got some kind of shielding. That's why it was so hard to find." His hands were flying across the panel.

Mance kept his voice calm, but firm. "We don't want to move it. Simply fix the Lift onto it, and keep it at maximum. If the detonator's electronic, we may be able to disrupt its magnetic field."

"Why didn't I think of that with the warhead!" Volk berated himself as he swiveled back around to the computer.

"Perhaps you had other things on your mind," Mance said gently, in part to himself.

"Maybe one of us should follow him down?" Shafus recommended.

Mance turned to him and said very diplomatically, "Let's not make matters any worse."

CHAPTER 22

The World's nuclear nightmare had taken a different twist by late that afternoon as the threatened deadline for detonation had come and past. Was there a bomb? No one knew, but the news broadcasts were filled with images of the steady stream of evacuees still leaving Jerusalem.

It was always possible that the bomb had been defective. It was also possible that it could go off in minutes. It might have been a cruel hoax, or a test, or just another form of ongoing terror.

Some thought it showed the terrorists had a heart, and that they were actually waiting for the city to empty. This was not an explanation the military entertained. But whatever the answer, the thousands who decided to stay in the Holy City and pray, and the many more who were unable to evacuate in time for the original deadline, were starting to think they might yet get a reprieve. Most were not going to tempt fate twice.

A strong shaft of sunlight entering the warehouse from a window above shown down on Jesus as he knelt in front of the truck. The back door was down and locked, but there was little doubt in Jesus' mind that he had found what he was looking for. Why the bomb did not explode, he could not say. All he knew was that he had prayed, and hoped, and that his prayers, so far, had been answered.

By this time the deadline was several hours past, and Jesus was feeling confident that the city was out of danger for the moment. He had nothing factual to base this on, but his instincts had always served him well in the past. He decided it was time he move his vigil out of doors, in the hope of attracting the authorities' attention so the bomb could be removed. He said one last prayer, and walked to the door.

When he emerged from the building he looked exhausted. He had been praying for several hours, and the circumstances had been terribly nerve wracking, even for someone not afraid of dying. Jesus looked around, then sat down next to the warehouse door to wait.

CHAPTER 23

In a dingy apartment looking more like a pawn shop than a residence, Dace, Kobra, and Basel watched the news reports in disbelief. Computers, electronics, tools, and weapons of every description were scattered everywhere, and even in the late afternoon, low hanging lights, which added to the dismal feel, were necessary for illumination.

That the bomb didn't detonate came as a shock, too much had gone into the planning. Dace, an avowed neo-Nazis had nearly completed a degree in Nuclear Physics at Ohio University before he was kicked out for illegal use of university computers. He had devised an ingenious, double-tier fail-safe system. In addition to its two primary, but separate, internal timer/detonators, it had infrared sensors to trigger it automatically if approached by intruders. So long as nothing could be traced, the operation would succeed, for if blame could not be fixed, they knew some terrorist group would happily grab the honor.

Years had gone into the planning, and millions spent on its execution. The components for the bomb were patiently assembled from a multitude of sources, purchased with hard currency, carefully laundered to avoid tracing. Even the terrorists were specially selected. Each was a loner, well educated, had deep personal grudges, usually with multiple political factions; and above all, an overwhelming desire to be rich.

The bombs Dace designed were perfect; compact, simple, and reliable. The Beirut bomb had already proven itself. So long as the bombs weren't discovered before they were set to explode, which had clearly been the case with the Jerusalem bomb, nothing could go wrong.

However, anticipating Wick's response to this latest development had the three terrorists filling the apartment with cigarette smoke. It wouldn't be long before they would be getting a call. But as to what their next move would be, they were still in the dark.

Andrew Barr felt like he had been strapped to the anchor desk ever since the Beirut story first broke. He had recently been divorced from his third wife, and he was grateful that he didn't have time to give it much thought. Ironically, that was the problem in the first place. The network practically demanded that family come second, and he had yet to meet anyone willing to put up with that for very long.

He had not taken much time to grieve over this new failure, though he did experience a twinge of sadness for not having children at this point in his life. But as Beirut unfolded, and each new day revealed another horror in the world, he began to feel it was probably for the best.

"… We take you live to the outskirts of Jerusalem and our Middle East correspondent, David Hiller."

"Andrew, I am at the Israeli Army observation and command post, nearly ten miles outside of Jerusalem. At this moment Israeli military leaders are trying to determine how long they should wait before sending men in, and what would be the safest way to search for the bomb while evacuating the remaining citizens."

"Everyone seems to have breathed a tremendous sigh of relief, but officials still caution people not to become overly optimistic. How long it would take to find a bomb, if there is a bomb, is anyone's guess at this point. The flip side is that if they don't find a bomb, how long will it be before the inhabitants of Jerusalem feel it's safe to return to the city?"

In the New York studio, Barr's camera flashed back on. He had received word via his earpiece of a Washington update: "What a mess. Thank-you, David. We will get back with you in a little while. We now go to our Washington correspondent, Sam Cohen. Sam?"

The image on the studio monitor shifted once again to an older reporter in suit and tie, standing on the steps of the U.S. Capital Building. It was already evening, but mobs of people, mostly reporters, lined the stairs.

Cohen had been the network's premier Washington correspondent for many years. Unflappable, he had one of those mellifluous voices that made the most horrendous occasions sound like the night before Christmas.

"Andrew, the President has called together an emergency meeting of the cabinet to discuss the situation. While everyone wishes that the entire ordeal would just blow over, no one is really expecting that to happen. Most of the world's major powers have put their military forces on full alert, but it's more symbolic than anything else since no one really knows who the culprits are at this point."

"Do they have any leads?" Barr asked from the studio.

"Not really," Cohen replied casually. "As expected, everyone is trying to get their share of the attention. There was even one report claiming it was the Irish Republican Army."

"Several pro-Iranian and Palestinian groups have threatened to carry these attacks out of the Middle East, to Europe and the United States. The government is taking these threats seriously, but they also caution the public to not become hysterical."

He looked straight at the camera for the big close. "One thing is very clear—There is a lot of money behind this operation. These devices are very expensive, and many here in Washington still favor the idea that this may be the work of some huge weapons cartel."

"What would lead them to suspect that?" Barr probed.

"In this case, a general lack of any information coming from the usual sources. Outside of these telephone calls, there's been a total lack of reliable information."

"Not terribly reassuring," Barr responded from the anchor's desk.

"No it isn't," Cohen said as his image was replaced by Barr's.

"We will get back to you in a little while, Sam." Barr turned to another camera that had found a new angle for the next segment of the story—How did average Americans feel about events in the Middle East? Barr hated the time-killing fillers.

CHAPTER 24

A large number of Israeli forces stood ready, but at a reasonably safe distance from Jerusalem. At the observation and command post, military brass and a few journalists huddled together in the sandbag bunker.

David Hiller had proven himself to the Israeli military on several occasions. While he took no sides, it was generally felt he tried his best to remain unbiased, and he was willing to follow the troops anywhere. Once, while traveling with an IDF patrol in South Lebanon, he had actually helped save two wounded soldiers after an ambush, at great risk to himself. He was extremely resourceful, and he did not get in the way, so it wasn't surprising to see him among the contingent.

The Israeli commander in charge of evacuating and securing Jerusalem was a general named Shimshelewitz. He scanned the major roads leading out of the city with binoculars, watching for signs of movement. With the exception of an occasional straggler, all was relatively quiet. He breathed a sigh of relief now that the evacuation was nearly complete.

A communications tent was set up several meters down the hill. An American colonel named Gordon emerged from the tent and was moving Shimshelewitz's direction. Gordon was assigned to act as liaison between the general and the American forces that were being deployed at the Israeli's request.

"General Shimshelewitz," Gordon said as he saluted.

"What is it, Colonel?"

"General Anderson's men are ready to move, sir."

Shimshelewitz took a deep breath before answering. "Very well. Let's see what we find." Gordon began moving back down the hill. "And Colonel…"

"Yes, sir?" Gordon turned back to him.

"Tell them to be careful."

"I will, sir."

A convoy of Israeli Army Humvees was moving toward the deserted city along the Hebron Road. Among them was the one carrying Lieutenant Aharon Reiss, and a young private named Singer.

Reiss was a meticulous soldier with a kind heart, and a good sense of humor. Deeply religious, he was a patriot, the type of person who would kill if he had to, while desperately hoping it would never come to that.

Singer was standing in the Humvees' top hatch opening, monitoring the needle on the Geiger counter which sat on the vehicle's roof, while holding the instrument's sensing tube high in the air. Singer was little more than a boy, but he had a good head on his shoulders, and Reiss was confident he could count on the young man if it should come to that.

As the Humvee rattled noisily along Reiss unholstered his pistol and laid it on the seat next to him. He yelled back to Singer over the sound of the wind and motor. "Keep your weapon ready. And don't hesitate to shoot if something seems suspicious."

"Shoot, sir?" Singer asked, thinking he may have misunderstood the order. Restraint was the word that he heard most often.

"General Shimshelewitz's orders. If there is a bomb that didn't detonate, chances are that whoever planted it will be trying to get to it as well."

Singer complied, reaching down and unholstering his sidearm and setting it on the roof next to the Gieger counter

CHAPTER 25

David Hiller had a good sense of the theatrical. Not only did he know a good story when he saw it, he knew exactly how to exploit it for all it was worth. As he prepared to let the world know of the latest developments in the hunt for the bomb, he noticed several helicopters in the distance flying toward the crest of the hill on which he was standing. Whereas other reporters might have waited for them to pass, Hiller would use them to get his audience's attention. Directing the cameraman who was working with him, he repositioned to take advantage of the incoming drama, and signaled for the camera to start recording.

"Andrew..." No sooner had Barr's name crossed Hiller's lips when three American helicopters overflew the bunker as they sped toward Jerusalem. Hiller could not have asked for better footage if he had requested it himself. The choppers passed by so close that Hiller felt compelled to duck, a cloud of dust kicking up around him. Another three shot past, and Hiller was in his glory. He shouted over the noise and desperately tried to hold onto his hat.

"Andrew, as you can see for yourself the military has decided to send in personnel to see if they can locate a bomb. Helicopters will be overflying the city with detection equipment, while troops in land vehicles will take to the streets. They'll also make sure that any stragglers they find are escorted safely out of the city."

The television's volume had been turned all the way down, but David Hiller's face was still on the screen, his hand still holding his hat. Wick sat silently for several moments before turning toward the three terrorists, who had been watching with him.

"Suggestions?" the man said, with more than a hint of threat.

The terrorists looked at each other. Finally Dace answered, his foot wiggling nervously. "We get back in there and see what the problem is. Set it off, or at least get it out of there."

"And just how do you propose to do that?" Wick responded angrily. "The place will be swarming with soldiers. There aren't any civilians left in the city. You'd stick out like sore thumbs!"

"No one said it was going to be easy," Kobra snapped back. She didn't like being pushed.

Wick made an imaginary gun with his hand and pointed it directly at her face. "No! You said it was fool proof! No mistakes!" He pulled the imaginary trigger, shooting her squarely in the forehead before dropping his hand. Dace, who never liked the man to begin with, stopped moving.

"It was foolproof! Just like the Beirut bomb," Basel said, not liking what he saw either. "Nothing could go wrong."

"Well, something went wrong!"

"There was redundancy built in at every level!" Dace yelled, smashing his cigarette into the ashtray, finally having enough. Being dressed down by some fat idiot who wasn't putting anything on the line was a little more than he could stomach. He shouted, his face almost exploding. "It was perfect!" The woman touched his arm. He looked at her, cooled a bit, then turned back to Wick. "There's no way that bomb wouldn't have fired. You understand? This shouldn't be happening!"

Wick drew his own anger inside. In truth he had been unnerved by Dace's explosion. He kept his voice down and even. "Well, it is happening, and if the people who are paying for this go down, be assured that we will all be going down with them. Now I suggest you get out, and do what you have to do! Find it, get it, or blow it up, I don't care, but fix it!"

The terrorists rose. Kobra and Basel moved toward the door, but Dace stopped in front of Wick and snarled menacingly. "I'm a bloody engineer, not your trigger man."

"You're a bloody killer," Wick responded in kind. "Now go and kill."

"Be careful I don't put a bomb under you," Dace sneered, tossing his cigarette at the man's silk shirt and tie. Wick leapt to his feet, shaking the burning embers from his clothes. He cursed Dace, but Dace and the other two had already left the room.

CHAPTER 26

Jesus was still sitting next to the old warehouse when he heard a frightening sound coming from overhead. He looked up just as several helicopters screamed past. They had been visible only a few seconds due to the height of the surrounding buildings, but the pounding, deafening, thumping of the rotors lingered long after. Suddenly he sensed that one of them was returning, and within seconds it was back, hovering overhead.

The sight of it sent chills running down his spine. Though he had seen helicopters during the information transfers aboard Resurrection, it did not prepare him for the real thing. It was as big as a house, and it was just hanging in air without any visible means of support, kicking up whirlwinds of dust. Jesus shielded his eyes.

The crew aboard the chopper had noticed increased fluctuation of the Geiger counter's needle as they passed over some old buildings. It wasn't much, but they had been instructed to check out every possibility, no matter how faint. As the pilot swung the chopper into position to observe the narrow street below, the copilot noticed a man standing up and brushing himself off. He seemed to be watching the helicopter, oblivious to the possible danger he might be in.

"Who is that?" the copilot yelled over the sound of the turbines.

"Some crackpot—I don't know," the pilot responded.

The copilot glanced back down at the Geiger counter. The needle's movement had increased dramatically. "Captain. This thing is going crazy! There's got to be something down there."

The pilot looked at the Geiger counter, then surveyed the situation outside. "The street's too narrow to set this thing down. Notify command. Tell them to get somebody on the ground over here fast. We'll hang around till then."

It wasn't long before a Humvee was driving up the street on which Jesus was still standing and watching the helicopter. Not until the chopper had finally flown off was he aware that he had other company.

The Humvee pulled up and stopped several doors away. Singer raised his weapon while Reiss grabbed his pistol, got out of the Humvee, and then motioned to Singer to hand him the Gieger counter. They eyed Jesus as he stood watching them. While he seemed harmless enough, his presence here was very odd, his demeanor almost too relaxed. It was always possible that he was carrying a weapon in the folds of his robe. Or worse—a detonator.

Reiss turned to Singer. "Stay there and cover me."

Reiss walked cautiously forward, keeping his pistol trained on Jesus the entire time. Jesus made no move, simply watching with curiosity. It was his first contact with a modern human.

Reiss stopped several yards away and yelled to Jesus in Arabic. "Put your hands over your head."

Jesus was slow to respond. He was aware that knowledge of modern Arabic was seeping into his consciousness, more information from the neural transfers, but it still took time to process.

"Now!" Reiss shouted. His voice brought Jesus back to the present. The Lieutenant was waving his gun, trying to indicate his intentions. Finally, Jesus raised his hands above his head.

Reiss started moving forward again, keeping his gun trained on Jesus the entire time. He took in every detail; clothes, skin color, beard, eyes. "You are a Palestinian Arab?" he guessed, still speaking in Arabic.

Jesus shook his head no. He had finally begun to remember.

"You're not Israeli?" Reiss said in disbelief, fooled by the robe.

This time Jesus responded out loud, and in English. "No, Jewish." Even he was surprised to hear these words.

"Don't be smart," Reiss responded, also in English. Though he had a good sense of humor normally, this was hardly the time or place for semantical jokes. And while he felt slightly more relaxed, he was keeping his pistol trained on Jesus nonetheless. "Walk to the Humvee and put your hands on the hood." He waved his pistol toward the vehicle.

Jesus complied without argument. He kept his movements slow and deliberate. He was not frightened, but he was cautious. He sensed Reiss meant him no harm.

"Spread your legs." Reiss moved Jesus' feet apart, motioned to Singer to cover him, then recalibrated the Geiger counter. When he ran the electrode over Jesus' clothes, the rate of clicking began to increase. He pointed it toward the building, and the clicks increased even more.

"What are you doing here?" Reiss questioned.

"There's a truck, in that building." Jesus motioned with his head. "The bomb is inside."

Reiss looked at Singer in disbelief. This man was either fearless, or a fool, and more than likely, a little of both.

Jesus started to turn around. "I had nothing to do with…"

"Put your hands back on the hood!" Singer screamed from his perch atop the Humvee. His voice and manner startled Jesus, who instantly complied. "You move again and I will kill you!"

Reiss walked toward the building, the noise from the Geiger counter increasing steadily, but still within the safety range. He pushed the door open with the muzzle of his pistol. His heart was racing. He turned back to Singer. "I'll be right back."

"Be careful, Lieutenant!" Singer yelled, keeping his weapon trained on Jesus.

Reiss disappeared inside the building.

The shafts of afternoon sunlight were still prominent in the dusty air as Reiss entered the warehouse. It was an ancient affair, and the smell of old wood and dust permeated his nostrils. As he stepped away from the door he saw the truck immediately.

He moved cautiously forward, scanning the building's interior, checking to make sure no one was hiding. He worked his way to the back of the vehicle, and found the sliding door down, and locked.

He gave considerable thought as to what to do next. Should he shoot the lock and find out what was inside? Should he leave it locked and call in the demolition experts? They would still have to get the lock off first. Then they might be killed. Then again, they might be able to cut it off, unless they could figure out the combination. His only means was to shoot it. He realized that he was going round and round out of fear, which was quite understandable of course, but it was not really getting him anywhere.

Surprising even himself, he aimed the gun to deliver a glancing shot, and thinking no further on the matter, held his breath and squeezed the trigger. The lock flew off, and he was still in one piece.

Outside the building, Singer was startled by the gunshot. Jesus had started to turn when, out of the corner of his eye, he saw Singer's pistol rise slightly. The two men stared at each other, unsure about what to do.

After a quick thank-you to whomever would listen, Reiss gently slid the door up. What he saw gave him pause. At the top of the assembly were two digital timers with wires running to separate detonators. The readouts on both timers were flickering very faintly: their numerical counters arrested at a very unsteady two seconds.

"Oh, my God!" Reiss whispered softly, moving away from the truck very slowly.

Reiss emerged from the building and walked briskly over to the Humvee. He threw his pistol on the passenger seat, and picked up a walkie-talkie.

"Checkpoint Bravo 3, this is Reiss, over." His voice was quivering as he spoke.

"Bravo three. Go ahead, Lieutenant," a voice shot back on the radio.

"Put General Shimshelewitz on."

Several seconds passed. Reiss nervously tapped the side of the radio, and Singer was starting to get a little antsy, not sure if he wanted to know what was going on or not.

"Shimshelewitz here. Go ahead, Lieutenant."

"Sir, we found the bomb."

Singer felt his knees go weak. "We did?" he whispered to himself. His pistol suddenly got ten pounds heavier.

"The bomb has two timers," Reiss continued. "Their numerical counters are blinking on and off, real faintly, but for some reason they both stopped at two seconds."

Singer couldn't believe what he was hearing. Why were they standing here chatting! He thought for sure he was going to vomit.

"Secure the area," the general instructed. "We'll get the specialists over there on the double."

"General, we've also got the man the chopper sighted in front of the building." Reiss glanced over at Jesus. "It's a little peculiar."

"Has he said anything?"

"Yes, sir. He told us where the bomb was."

"Do we know who he is?"

"I'll check, sir." Reiss moved to Jesus. "Who are you? Do you have any identification?"

Jesus shook his head.

Reiss pressed the button down on the walkie-talkie. "No, sir. He claims to be an Israeli. And he speaks English."

"You're right about it being peculiar, Lieutenant. Go on and bring him in and we'll check him out here."

"Yes, sir." Then he quickly added," Tell them to hurry, General."

"I'll do that, Lieutenant. Good work." The radio was silent.

Reiss dropped the walkie-talkie from his ear. A visible sweat broke out on his face. He moved away from Jesus, rounding the front of the vehicle, studying the man's eyes. There was something about them, but Reiss couldn't put his finger on what it was.

As Reiss approached the driver's side he signaled to Singer to stay alert, then turned to Jesus.

"Get in."

Perhaps it was the arbitrary motion of his hand waving emptily in space, but Reiss suddenly realized he had no gun. He immediately reached for his holster only to find it empty as well. Then his eyes flashed to the pistol laying on the passenger seat.

By the time Reiss realized what had happened Jesus was already stepping into the vehicle, while Singer lowered himself back into the Humvee keeping his sidearm trained on the man. Oddly enough, Jesus found himself quite excited by the thought of taking his first ride in such a machine. As he began to settle down into the seat, he noticed Reiss' gun. Without thinking, he reached for it to move it aside.

"Lieutenant!" Singer shouted as he pulled the trigger.

A shot rang out and Jesus slumped forward in his seat.

CHAPTER 27

Could the Resurrections' disruption of the energy field around the bomb really have worked? Several hours had passed and Jerusalem was still intact, but there was no way for the Kels to know for sure. It was possible that the bomb's failure to explode had been the result of faulty design, or it may have simply been a hoax. It was a crazy world, and anything was possible. As a result, the aliens decided to keep the Lift focused on the weapon until they heard unequivocally that it was found, and disarmed. Now the problem was: Where was Jesus?

Shafus and Mance were in the control room listening to news broadcasts, hoping for any piece of information that might disclose his whereabouts. Volk was fussing with the ship's sensing equipment, but he held out little hope for success.

The room had the feeling of a funeral parlor until Mance finally broke the silence. He was communicating the information that he was getting over his headset. "They found the bomb…" He paused, waiting for the next bit of news, "and a man…" He stopped and turned to the others. "They said they had to shoot him."

Shafus' eyes dropped right to the floor.

"I had him located before," Volk said. "We should have sent someone down. Now there's nothing…"

Shafus looked at Mance, still thinking about the report. "It could have been someone else, don't you think?"

Mance did not respond, and Shafus felt shame once he realized what he was suggesting.

"Shall I turn the sensors off?" Volk inquired of Mance.

"Yes. Turn them off. He could be anywhere at this point."

"Couldn't we send someone down to search for him?" Shafus implored.

"It's too risky," Mance answered. "For the time being we will listen. We're bound to hear more about it."

CHAPTER 28

Reiss and Singer had mixed feelings when they saw the bomb squad pull up. Reiss worried that their tampering might end up setting it off. He remembered someone saying, if it's not broken, don't fix it. He wasn't sure if that applied in this case or not.

The team of six entered the warehouse, their Geiger counters clicking. They rounded the back of the truck, its sliding door still open, and peered inside, hardly breathing. They had disarmed many a bomb, and normally size didn't matter. When your body was being torn apart, the magnitude of the explosion was pretty irrelevant. But this was different. Not only were their own lives on the line, it was quite feasible that many others might be killed as well. It would all depend on the yield of the bomb, but by assuming it was at least a close copy of the Beirut bomb, they had a fairly accurate estimate. It was unfortunate that the blueprint had been destroyed, since homemade bombs usually reflected some idiosyncrasy of the designer's personality. What that might be in this case was anybody's guess, so they would need to proceed with extreme caution.

The other issue was Jerusalem itself. Its history, antiquities, its very being represented the best, and worst, in man. How would the world react if this holiest of places actually disappeared. They were determined not to finish the terrorists' job for them, but one look at the bomb, with its double timer and detonating systems made them realize it would probably not be easy to do.

Once they actually climbed into the truck and moved toward the bomb, their problems seemed to compound. They felt light-headed, woozy, and on edge, and could only stand to be near it for short intervals of time. It was as if something were disrupting their nervous systems. What's more, none of their instruments or motor driven tools would work properly. Anything that used electrical current; sensors, relays, computers, even the Geiger counters, simply would not function when brought into close proximity with the bomb. Outside the truck they would be fine, while inside they would cease to function.

At first they did not know if this was part of the overall design, or attributable to some other factor. But when they discovered the bomb's infrared sensor, and deduced its probable function, they reasoned that the anomaly had not been intentional. As scientists they were curious about what was causing the phenomenon, and at that point extremely grateful for its existence, light-headedness and all, but discussion would have to wait until later.

In the end, the solution was very simple. After hours of frustration, and trying everything they could think of, they relied on the only implements which seemed to work. They assumed that since no electricity was flowing, the chance of triggering any self-protective fail-safe system was minimal, so they went ahead. A few snips later, just minutes after the decision had been made, the bomb was disarmed; thanks to pliers, a screwdriver, and a wirecutter. So much for technology.

Lieutenant Reiss breathed a huge sigh of relief as he and Singer headed out of the city toward the command post. But something kept nagging at him as he drove. It was something that one of the bomb experts had said to him before they headed out, his hand quivering as he spoke—"You know, we should all be dead."

CHAPTER 29

Jesus opened his eyes and found himself in a room that vaguely reminded him of the life functions center on board Resurrection. While it did not seem as technical, nor modern as the ship's facility, it certainly was as clean. He knew immediately he was in a hospital.

He rolled his head toward the windows and saw a nurse sitting in the light of the afternoon, reading. An attractive woman in her late twenties, Nurse Kafni put down her book and moved to the bed as soon as she realized he had stirred.

She communicated with only a smile, reaching for the panel above the headboard. It was only seconds after she pressed the button that a voice called out over the intercom.

"Yes?"

"Please tell Dr. Franklin his patient is awake." Kafni released the button, picked up Jesus' wrist, stared at her watch for several seconds, wrote something down on the chart at the end of the bed, then returned to wrap his arm with a cuff to take his blood pressure.

Jesus watched, not saying a word. He was still feeling very groggy.

The nurse let the air out of the cuff, recorded her findings, then finally broke the silence.

"How are you feeling?"

"Very sleepy." His speech was somewhat slurred.

She smiled. "I would expect so. You've been unconscious for almost a week now."

"What happened?" he said, trying to move, but finding himself in too much pain to do so. "Where am I?"

"All in due time."

The nurse moved to the side as the door to the hospital room swung open and two doctors entered, one male, one female. They took up stations on opposite sides of the bed.

"It's good to see you back in the world of the living."

The male, Doctor Franklin, was the first to address him. While he may have been attempting to exhibit a warm bedside manner, there was an awkwardness about him that prohibited genuine contact. "We didn't know if you would make it for awhile there. I'm Doctor Franklin, this is Doctor Mazar." he said, referring to the female doctor.

Doctor Mazar smiled and moved toward the bed, careful not to get too close and frighten the patient. Since she knew nothing about him at this point, she wanted first and foremost to establish a level of trust.

"I'm going to check your pupil response, is that okay?"

Jesus nodded. In his half waking mind, it seemed his life was becoming an endless series of experiences that were being lived over and over, only each time with a different cast of characters. He was beginning to doubt whether anything was real.

Dr. Mazar took out a small penlight and proceeded with her examination. The touch of her hand on his forehead was soothing, and he found himself unavoidably looking directly into her eyes. She clicked the light off, finding her connection to him difficult to break, though she did not acknowledge it openly. Realizing that it might appear awkward, she forced herself to turn away and address Doctor Franklin.

"His pupil response looks normal," she said, a slight hesitation in her voice.

"His vitals are all strong too, Doctor," Nurse Kafni added from where she stood.

"Excellent." Doctor Franklin rubbed his hands together. He seemed very uncomfortable. "I'm not going to ask how you're feeling because I have a pretty good idea. For the moment it's best that you sleep. Nurse Kafni will stay in the room with you should you need anything." His voice took on a slightly more serious tone. "When you're feeling better, there are some gentlemen who would like to ask you a few questions. Do you understand?"

"I understand." Jesus looked around the room. All were staring at him, but saying nothing. "Would someone please tell me what happened?"

The two doctors exchanged nervous glances.

"You were shot," Franklin said, finally speaking up. "One of the soldiers who picked you up saw you go for a weapon. You were brought to this hospital in Tel Aviv. You are lucky to be alive."

Jesus looked at him. He remembered nothing of the shooting.

"You had better rest now," Doctor Mazar said softly. "You'll be able to talk more later." She turned to Nurse Kafni. "Let us know immediately if anything changes."

"Of course, Doctor."

"And don't get any ideas about escaping," Franklin suddenly added.

"They've posted guards on this entire wing, and throughout the hospital."

As Mazar and Franklin left the room Jesus was wondering what prompted the doctor to say such a thing. At the moment he couldn't even sit up. He looked back toward the window and saw the nurse smile at him before sinking back into her book. Giving in to his condition, he closed his eyes and immediately drifted back to sleep.

For Doctor Mazar and Doctor Franklin it had been a very trying week. The hospital had been turned into a militarized zone, as well as a zoo. Reporters and soldiers were posted at every entrance, even the fire exits. Each trip to work was a marathon of security checks and questions, for which there were usually no answers.

The reasons there were no answers varied. In some cases it was the truth. In other cases, they had been ordered by the military not to say anything. Everything had to go through government censors. Lastly, there were a few things that only Franklin and Mazar knew at this point, and they were afraid to tell anyone, especially the military.

It was a game of cat and mouse, and it seemed like everyone was angry with them. The general public assumed the patient had had a hand in the nuclear attack on Beirut, and were angry at the doctors for protecting him. The reporters were angry because they were being denied full access to a good story. The military was convinced the doctors were stalling and being overly protective. Even the hospital administrators were starting to buckle under the pressure. Franklin and Mazar were under siege, and the situation was about to get worse.

As they left Jesus' room and stepped into the corridor they saw Colonel Gordon coming down the hall at a good clip.

"Here comes trouble!" Franklin whispered under his breath.

His response belied his true feelings, but the situation was complex. In a way they were anxious to see the military take charge of the patient. The monkey would finally be off their backs; they could get on with their lives, and just be doctors. Neither was enjoying the limelight.

On the other hand, they were in no way prepared for this encounter yet. When they received word that Jesus was conscious, they asked the duty nurse to call the colonel and inform him as to the patient's status. That's all. Leave it to the military to be prompt Mazar thought to herself.

They were sure the American colonel was not going to like what they had to say. Indeed, they wondered if they would even have their positions at the hospital in a couple of hours. They both took a deep breath as he approached.

"I got your message," Gordon said amiably as he walked up. "I came as soon as I could."

"It was not really necessary," Franklin said, a hint of irritation seeping through. "We just wanted you to know he appeared to be out of danger."

"I misunderstood," the colonel said apologetically.

"It will be a day or two before he will be coherent enough to answer any questions," Franklin went on.

"Did he say anything?"

"He wanted to know what had happened," Doctor Mazar responded. "I don't think he remembered any of it."

"He was severely traumatized," Franklin added.

"Any idea about who he is?"

"No. It's a total mystery." Mazar tried her best to not sound evasive, but she had never considered herself a good actor.

"We have a few more mysteries of our own to add."

"Such as," Gordon asked, a hint of skepticism already creeping into his voice.

Franklin had fired the first shot. He looked over at Mazar as if to say, are you ready? She wasn't, but then she'd never be, so why not dive right in she thought.

"Did you notice his wrists when they brought him in?" Franklin asked cautiously, feeling his way along.

"No." The colonel's flat response left little doubt that this was not going to be easy.

"Scars," Franklin continued. "Puncture wounds. And a pair to match on his feet. Nasty things, went right through the bones. We X-rayed them."

"All completely healed," Mazar tossed in, her eyebrows raised, and her head shaking gently up and down.

"What's the point?" The colonel seemed completely clueless. Franklin wondered if he was a good poker player.

"It's the kind of wound you would expect to find on a person who was crucified." There. Franklin had said it. He waited for a response. It took a few seconds, but the colonel finally put the pieces together.

"Oh, come on, Doctor. Who are you trying to kid?"

Mazar jumped in this time, and without reservations. Her professional integrity was now on the line. "We can document everything we say, Colonel. Including a gash in his side, caused by a long sharp object…"

"A knife, or perhaps a spear," Franklin interjected.

Mazar continued. "Whatever the object, it definitely penetrated his heart. There is scar tissue to prove it."

"Of course, that too is miraculously healed," Franklin added, a part of him having trouble believing what he was saying. "Add to that, scars the entire circumference of his scalp…"

Gordon finally blew. "Are you two crazy! Listen to what you're saying." He paused to gather himself together and settle down. He didn't know if he wanted to laugh, or scream. He admonished the two doctors. "At best it's coincidence. Or a setup. We don't have to fall for it. It's time for a reality check here, Doctors." He started to walk away.

"Let us show you the X-rays," Doctor Mazar pleaded, following him down the hall.

He turned to her. "I'm sorry. I've got no more time for this. Call me when he's able to talk. Good day, Doctors."

Gordon left them standing in the hall. They were totally drained, feeling like children who had just been spanked. Franklin looked at Mazar.

"Frankly, I'm not so sure he isn't right."

CHAPTER 30

The terrorists were back in their hole. It was night, and they sat at a small table under a lone hanging lamp.

"We've got to get to that bomb." Basel said, knowing full well that he had not the vaguest idea of how this might be accomplished.

"You're dreaming," Dace scoffed, his foot shaking incessantly. "It's deep in some building being inspected piece-by-piece by Israelis, Americans, Brits, and every other bloody government in the world, and it's got our fingerprints all over it! No! What we've got to do is to leave. Now!"

"They'll kill us if we just take off!" Basel argued, referring to their bosses.

"They'll kill us if we don't," Dace responded, referring to the Israelis. He got up and moved away from the table.

"We need a diversion." Kobra lit a fresh cigarette from the one she was already smoking. She had been sitting back, thinking, formulating a plan. "Why don't we try to get our hands on the man they found with the bomb instead?"

"For what?" Dace said bluntly, not thinking much of the idea.

"Because a lot of fools think he's Jesus Christ," the woman said coolly.

"You don't believe that?" Basel said, laughing out loud.

She looked at him and sneered, "It's not what I believe that matters."

CHAPTER 31

There was no way to keep the rumors from spreading under such volatile circumstances. The staff attending Jesus had been kept to a minimum, but it was still large enough to create monumental security problems. Talk spread through any hospital like wildfire. What's more, the horror surrounding Beirut, and the euphoria over Jerusalem's reprieve had turned the reporters into ravenous wolves, scrapping for details. The beleaguered staff often found themselves tricked out of information, or throwing out morsels just to keep the pack at bay. Thus, little-by-little, the stories began to grow.

The hospital staff was left to speculate as to their patient's identity. Fully aware that he might be a terrorist, they were nonetheless drawn to him, all trying to make sense of the scars he carried. As word of these spread, hospital workers sought ways they might sneak a peek for themselves, some not very discreet. While outwardly the notion that he might be the Savior was ridiculed, many a heart was secretly hoping that this was the miracle the world so desperately needed.

Doctors Franklin and Mazar finally gave Colonel Gordon the go ahead. A short time later Gordon, and his commander, General Anderson, were approaching the hospital entrance on foot. They were accompanied by Lieutenant Reiss, whose presence it was felt, might be useful should it be necessary to jog the prisoner's memory.

Reiss was glad he had been ordered to accompany them for private reasons. He had been worried about the prisoner's well being. He had seen something in his eyes, and while Reiss' Jewish upbringing dismissed the silly idea that this man was Christ, he knew in his heart that the man had meant him no harm.

As the three officers climbed the front steps the reporters encircled them with cameras and microphones. The soldiers who formed the hospital security detachment rushed to aid Anderson, Gordon, and Reiss as they bulldozed their way through amid the flurry of questions.

"Any idea who he is, General?" one reporter yelled.

"Do you suspect he planted the bomb and planned to die in the blast?" another pleaded.

"Is he a Palestinian, General? Does he have connections with the Iranians or Iraqis?"

Lieutenant Reiss ushered reporters out of the way as he helped the general to the door. "Please, step aside."

"Come on, General. Give us some answers," one reporter cried mournfully. Anderson actually felt a tinge of sympathy.

"Gentlemen, I wish I had answers to give you. Unfortunately, the man has been in isolation since the incident. All I know at this point is it's a hot issue the Israelis have asked the Americans to handle."

"Why?" a voice shot back from the crowd. "Why have Americans been brought in?" It was definitely an Israeli, and clearly hostile.

"As soon as we get any information, we will pass it along to you," Anderson said evasively.

"Do you think he is responsible for the Beirut bombing, General?"

Anderson shot a quick look over at Gordon and then back at the reporters. "We are investigating the possibility." He turned to leave.

"General, we've heard constant rumors that this man has some very interesting, how shall I put it—scars? Any truth to these reports?"

This was one rumor that Anderson was determined to crush if at all possible. He knew that if it got out of hand it could ignite an already precarious world. In addition, he personally found the thought thoroughly repugnant. He turned on the reporters, staring at them, his eyes absolutely frigid—"None! Obviously a hoax invented by some sick and overly active mind. Now, if you will excuse us ladies and gentlemen, maybe we can get some answers to your questions."

The soldiers who were stationed at the door snapped to attention when the three officers entered the ward a few minutes later. The flurry startled Doctor Franklin who was standing at the station desk, reviewing charts. He would be supervising the interrogation by himself since Doctor Mazar was catching up on badly needed sleep.

Anderson seemed amiable enough when he greeted Doctor Franklin. If Gordon had related the conversation he'd had with the doctors a few days earlier, the general certainly wasn't letting on. It was possible the general simply didn't care, but somehow Franklin thought this very unlikely. Like all Israelis, Franklin had done his military service, and he knew generals didn't get to be generals without a bit of caginess. He assumed Anderson was simply not tipping his hand, and it would behoove Franklin to remain cautious.

"Quite a zoo out there," the general commented as he extended his hand to the physician.

"Yes it is," Doctor Franklin said amiably.

"We got your call about coming to question him. Is that still acceptable with you?"

"Yes," Franklin responded. "He's much stronger now, though I will need to accompany you so I can keep an eye on him. If I feel like the questioning is becoming too much for him, I will request you stop."

"Of course. You're the doctor, Doctor." Anderson couldn't wait until the Army got full control.

"This way, gentlemen." Franklin lead the three men across the hall and motioned for them to wait. He knocked on the door and then entered by himself. A few seconds later he returned and waved the others in.

Jesus was sitting upright when the men entered. Nurse Kafni had just finished raising the bed and fluffing the pillows. She was becoming quite fond of Jesus, and the officers' stern faces made her feel very protective. Doctor Franklin motioned for her to leave the room as he stepped to the far side of the bed. She complied, but not happily.

"These are the men I told you about," Doctor Franklin said quietly to Jesus. "They want to ask a few questions. You're sure you feel up to it?"

"I think so." Jesus nodded politely and smiled.

"Good." Franklin turned and began the introductions. "This is General Anderson of the American Army, Commander of the U.S. contingent in Israel." The general put his hat down on a bureau near the door and stepped stiffly forward, giving Jesus only the slightest nod of recognition. "His aid, Colonel Gordon, also an American." Gordon gave a cursory smile. "And Lieutenant Reiss," Franklin continued, "an officer in the Israeli Army."

"Yes. I remember you." Jesus studied Reiss' eyes for a moment. "You were one of the soldiers who found me."

"Yes. I'm sorry you were shot. When you reached for my pistol the private feared for my life."

"Of course," Jesus responded gently. "It was my fault. I am not used to guns. It had not even occurred to me."

"How could it not occur to you? How could somebody live in Jerusalem these days and not have at least some familiarity with weapons and what they mean?" The general's manner was brash as he grabbed the offensive.

"How do some people live their entire lives in this world and never notice the beauty that surrounds them? What one cares about is a matter of choice." Jesus had hoped to deflect the question with a tempered response, but he sensed he had rubbed Anderson the wrong way. No matter, the general's attitude had been surly. Jesus would have to take care to keep his temper in check.

"You speak English very well," Gordon said, trying to cut some of the escalating tension. "Where did you learn?"

"I speak many languages. Jerusalem is the center of the world for many cultures, as you know."

"What's your name?" Anderson pressed on.

"I told the doctors, I cannot say."

"Can't? Or won't?" the general demanded.

"Can't." He studied the general for a moment. "Perhaps I will be able to tell you in the future."

"That's crap!" the general snapped. "You'll tell me now!" His voice got lower and he moved in closer, leaning over the bed rail. "Don't think you can be clever with me, because it won't work. Over a half million people lost their lives, and I will not play games with you. Is that understood!"

Jesus stared at the man, but said nothing. The general was right, Jesus was being evasive, but he was certain the whole truth would not improve the current situation. The general was not very receptive at the moment, and one mention of the word 'alien' would have driven him right over the top.

As the general leaned against the bed waiting for a response, his eye caught sight of Jesus' wrist. The doctors had been right, they were nasty wounds. He raised Jesus' arm as he spoke, examining the scar more closely.

"The doctors informed my adjutant about your previous injuries. They described them as potentially life threatening. They said you have a scar on the side of your rib cage. A remnant of a wound that should have proved fatal."

"A scratch. I've had it for many, many years."

Anderson put Jesus' hand back on the bed. "I was told it was relatively recent," he said accusingly, "and much more than a scratch! The wound seems to have penetrated your heart, yet somehow you managed to live. How could that happen?"

"God was not ready for me to die, I suppose."

The general smacked his forehead in a theatrical show of self-mockery. "Oh, I see. Of course. How stupid of me." His voice became cynical, sharp, and insulting. "No name, no identification, potentially fatal wounds which are perfectly healed, puncture wounds on your wrists and feet. To top it all off, you sit nonchalantly outside of a building which contains a thermonuclear bomb! Foolproof! That is how it was described to me. Foolproof! Even the experts don't know what kept the thing from going off. But I thank God it didn't! And I have a hunch that you didn't expect to be here today, and these scars are just a cover in case the plan didn't go the way it was supposed to."

Jesus could not help grinning. "The General is very creative."

Anderson got nose-to-nose with Jesus. "I don't know who you are or where you came from, but I know you're an extremist, and I'm going to figure out who you belong to. Do you understand me? This whole thing is a setup! And we're going to find out who is behind it!"

"I hope you do, General." Jesus was unruffled. "But as for me, I assure you, I mean no one any harm, and I had nothing to do with the bomb. If anything, I would like to go back and assist those who have been forced from their homes because of this tragedy. I would recommend you do the same. You might find you had fewer questions, and more answers."

"Don't you dare take that...."

Dr. Franklin broke in, quickly injecting himself between the general and Jesus. "Gentlemen, I don't think this conversation is getting us anywhere, nor do I think it is good for the patient. He is still in a very weakened condition. It may account for the vagueness of some of his responses." He shot a stern glance back at Jesus. "Perhaps in a few days we could have another go at it."

General Anderson grabbed his hat, then turned to the doctor. "Perhaps? There is no perhaps about it. We will get to the bottom." The general stared at Jesus, his eyes cold with hatred, then left the room ahead of the other officers.

Gordon thanked Franklin, then followed. Reiss, however, lingered. He studied Jesus for several seconds, then wished him "Good luck," before leaving the room.

Franklin waited a moment for the door to close, then lowered the bed a little. "You could have been more cooperative. They're just trying to prevent more killing."

"So am I, Doctor Franklin."

Dr. Franklin shook his head. He realized he no longer had any doubts. Whatever else he might be, this man was not a terrorist.

CHAPTER 32

The media's continual coverage of events in the aftermath of Beirut, as well as what had been dubbed the "Miracle of Jerusalem" had one distinct advantage for the aliens, they now always knew where Jesus was. The press had been infuriated after Anderson's meeting with Jesus, when told he had nothing new to tell them. They were certain Anderson was stonewalling, but in point of fact, he wasn't.

That afternoon Shafus, Mance, Volk and Kaseel held a meeting in the ship's lounge to discuss the idea of sending Kaseel to the surface, but the plan made Mance very nervous. He was certain that getting to Jesus would prove very dangerous, leaving them with a bigger problem than they had right now.

For Shafus, the decision was more difficult because he now viewed Jesus as a member of the crew. "We have lost control of the situation, Mance. We must get Jesus up to the ship."

Mance sensed Shafus was losing his sense of objectivity. "We have never had control of this situation, Shafus," Mance said gently, "and he is in the hands of qualified physicians." Mance knew they must let things find their own time and way now. This may not have been the way they envisioned things happening, but events were in motion, and there was no reason to stop them at this point.

"All the news reports indicate that he is holding his own," Volk added optimistically.

Mance nodded. "Jesus, I have observed, is quite capable of taking care of himself." He put his hand on Shafus' shoulder. "For the moment, we will stay alert. If the right opportunity presents itself, we will try to have Kaseel get a locator to him. Agreed?"

Mance's calm and diplomatic assurance eased some of Shafus' concerns. It was agreed.

CHAPTER 33

Jesus was getting stronger with each passing day. Though the medical care he got at the hospital was not nearly as sophisticated as what he received on board the Resurrection, it was more than adequate, and his pain was much more tolerable. But with his recovery came the realization that he needed to formulate a plan. While the information acquired by the time buoys had been very complete, learning about a society through neural transfers, and actually participating in it, were two different things entirely.

Jesus had taken to watching the television in his hospital room, and was fascinated by the steady barrage of information, and misinformation. He could also see that getting away from reporters was going to be a near impossibility. He observed, close-up, how the rules of social engagement had changed since Roman times, and the thought of navigating this new maze seemed rather daunting. He prayed for help.

He was just finishing when Nurse Kafni entered with Doctor Franklin. Jesus immediately switched off the television, as it turned out, right in the middle of a commercial. Somehow he had not gotten used to having reports about atrocities interrupted by people with smiling faces trying to sell various products.

As Franklin reviewed his charts Jesus wondered how much longer he would have to stay. Things were starting to feel a little too comfortable, and that was always a danger. It was tempting to play it safe, but that had never been his way, and he was not about to start doing that now.

Similar questions were running through Franklin's mind. The doctor knew there was little reason to keep the patient much longer, but he was concerned about what would happen once he signed the medical release. To his way of thinking, Jesus was starting to look like a sacrificial lamb, and it was hard to know who would get the lion's share of the carcass, media or military.

"How are you feeling this morning?" Nurse Kafni said as she tidied up the room.

"I'm fine. Much better today actually."

Jesus addressed Doctor Franklin, who had begun checking the dressing on his wound. "How much longer must I stay?"

"As far as I'm concerned, you should be able to leave very soon." Franklin continued to work. "You'll need to come back every few days to have the dressing changed. Other than that, the wound is healing very nicely." He stepped away and looked at Jesus, wearing a slight frown.

Jesus studied him for a moment. "I sense some reservation on your part."

Franklin ducked the question. "Colonel Gordon is here from General Anderson's office. He wants to talk with you. Shall I let him in?"

"Yes, I will talk with him." Jesus was still waiting for an answer.

"Nurse Kafni, will you send Colonel Gordon in please."

"Yes, Doctor."

Franklin felt trapped in a tangle of conflicting feelings. The anger he felt over the bombing of Beirut made him want to help the government insure that nothing like it ever happened again. At the same time, his gut told him that this man was not the problem, and perhaps might even be the answer. He wanted to offer advice, but he had no idea what to say. All he could ultimately do, was try to make the situation easier on everyone.

Jesus could see the anguish on Franklin's face. "I wish there was something I could do to help. Something I could say."

The doctor thought for a moment. "I don't know what is going to happen, but I hope you will be honest with him. Make it easy on yourself. That's all."

"I appreciate your advice, Doctor. I will endeavor to answer all the colonel's questions as honestly as I can."

The doctor fixed his eyes on Jesus' eyes, not breaking the lock until Colonel Gordon entered the room.

"Good morning," Gordon said cheerfully. He had decided to start with a whole new tact.

"Good morning, Colonel Gordon."

"How are you feeling?" Gordon asked from the foot of the bed.

"Much better, thank-you."

"I was just telling our patient that from a doctor's standpoint, he is just about ready to go home."

"Wherever that might be." Gordon realized he was just about to nuke his new strategy, but, he rationalized, it was the doctor who had opened up this can of worms.

"Can you tell me that?" he pressed on. "Or has your memory been wiped selectively clean?"

"I don't know what you mean?" Jesus said innocently.

"I mean you remember what you want to. Like the various languages you speak…"

"Actually," Franklin interjected quickly, "it is common in cases of amnesia for patients to retain their memory of language."

"But you did recognize Lieutenant Reiss, and you met him before you were shot I believe. Isn't that so?"

Jesus said nothing, neither confirming, nor denying.

Gordon went on. "All we want is some straight answers to a few questions. If they're satisfactory, you're free to go. If not, well, I'm not sure what will happen. A lot of people died in Beirut. If you had nothing to do with it, answer our questions and just stay out of the way. Believe me, you don't want to become more deeply involved."

Colonel Gordon's tone of voice had been firm, but respectful. He had integrity, and Jesus found himself liking the man. He seemed to be doing his best to be forthright. Jesus wanted to do the same, but he didn't know if Gordon was going to accept what he had to say.

"Colonel Gordon, so many people are killed and your advice to me is not to become more deeply involved?" Jesus shook his head, but his voice remained gentle. "Why would I do that? What could possess me? How could one possibly stay—uninvolved? How do people in this society distance themselves from such incredible suffering?"

"Don't carry your self-righteous act too far," Gordon reprimanded, some of his composure fading. "It seems to me you may be the biggest and sickest hoax to come out of this tragedy yet."

Jesus had heard accusations like this before, but this one cut deep. He felt as though the wind were knocked out of him. "What do you mean?"

"Well, you're Jesus Christ, right? Isn't that what the world is supposed to believe?" The colonel gave a twisted little laugh. "Did you really think we were that stupid?"

"Colonel…"

"You may have duped some of the world, but you haven't fooled everyone. We know this masquerade was costly, and money can be traced, as well as procedures. There are only a handful of doctors in the world that could manage this. What we don't understand is what you hoped to accomplish? Who was behind it? The Russians?"

"No one was behind anything."

"Were you going to talk us out of our commitment to defend Israel?" He waited for a response, but Jesus said nothing. Gordon peered at him intensely. "You've been discovered. There's nothing to gain by concealing the truth."

"Colonel, I am not trying to conceal a thing. I simply don't think you would believe what I have to tell you."

"Try me!" Gordon pleaded.

"No government on Earth is behind this." Jesus wondered what he could say to convince this man. He looked Gordon straight in the eye. "I have had no operations to make me appear this way. My name is Jesus. I come from Nazareth. I am a carpenter, a Rabbi, and a peaceful man."

"How did you get here?"

"I was born here. How did you get here?"

Gordon was not in the mood for games. A bit of anger started bleeding into his voice. "I mean, how did you get to this time?"

"I was brought here."

"How? By whom?"

"I cannot tell you." Jesus sat quietly.

Gordon had had enough. "I won't even dignify this conversation with a response. As far as I'm concerned you are a ridiculous fraud who deserves exactly what you are going to get."

"I have no fear, Colonel."

"Good, because here's what's coming down. Since we're sure you're not the one who built the bomb, and that your involvement in the affair is peripheral, General Anderson has left it to my discretion. I can recommend to the Israelis that they turn you loose—if I see fit." His voice got deep, intense, personal. "You see, your little joke has gone a bit too far. Now the world wants to know more about you, and they won't stop asking questions until they've milked you dry. The military has enough problems without playing into your game. Let your public crucify you, we wash our hands of it. The truth will come out eventually, and with your notoriety, you won't be hard to find."

"What convinces you that my purpose here is destructive? Can't you sense what's in my heart?"

"Quite honestly, all I sense is a sick individual who stands for nothing, and whom I despise." Gordon could feel his hatred welling up inside him. He wanted to cry, and shout, but fought for composure. "Your kind makes a mockery of religion. Out of life itself. You make me sick." He moved toward the door, then turned to Doctor Franklin. "I will call you as soon as this clears with the I.D.F. and General Anderson."

He looked at Jesus one more time. "You know, the general was too disgusted to see you again. I understand. Just wait. There must be five hundred reporters downstairs. Informational sharks. If you are Jesus, welcome to the real world." Gordon turned and left the room.

"Well, Jesus," Doctor Franklin said as soon as the door had shut behind the colonel, "it looks like you're a free man."

CHAPTER 34

It took a full day to get official authorization from Israel's government and process the paperwork for Jesus' release. No matter what their private feelings were on the matter, for obvious reasons, prudence demanded the Israelis distance themselves from this situation. While their investigation would continue, the rising storm of protest was too strong to justify holding this man.

General Anderson was furious, but public sentiment had backed him into a corner. The American military had been christened the AmeRoman Legion in political cartoons around the world. A caricature of Anderson sporting a Roman sword, sandals, and centurion helmet with plume, stung the devout Southern Baptist deeply. With pressure mounting, he capitulated, and decided to set the man free, but vowed to make the event so public that the charlatan could not hope to avoid exposure. He used the extra day to set his plan in motion.

Doctor Franklin had been pondering what he had heard during the interview with Colonel Gordon. He still found no resolution to his dilemma. Who could possibly believe that this man was Jesus Christ? And if it were so, why would Franklin, an Israeli Christian, an ordinary doctor, be the one chosen by God to care for this man? It all made no sense, yet he had developed such an overwhelming fondness.

Nurse Kafni had Jesus packed and the wheelchair ready by the time Franklin and Doctor Mazar entered the room to see their patient off. The nurse's concern was evident, but she never let her smile sag. She helped him into the wheelchair, and handed him the little bag of items he had received from the hospital—his only possessions.

"Thank you all for your kindness."

"What will you do? Where will you go?" Franklin asked.

"I will go to the hospital entrance with Nurse Kafni, and then I will put one foot in front of the other and see where it takes me, just like I always have." He smiled.

"Answer one thing for me," Franklin asked, clearly troubled. "Are you really…" His question seemed like such an absurdity that he stopped mid-sentence.

"Yes. I am," Jesus responded, knowing full well what the doctor wanted to know. Franklin bowed his head. Jesus looked back at Nurse Kafni. "I'm ready." The nurse wheeled him to the door.

"Good luck."

Jesus looked back at Doctor Mazar. "Thank-you."

Nurse Kafni and Jesus received an armed escort to the hospital lobby. They could see through the glass that it was total bedlam outside. It appeared General Anderson had been successful in his efforts.

One of the soldiers helped Jesus from the wheelchair, allowing him little more than a glance back at the nurse before being ushered out of the building.

As he approached the outer door Jesus could not only see the chaos, he could begin to hear it. Thousands of people stood on the hospital grounds chanting, screaming, yelling, and waving placards of support, and protest. And there were reporters, hundreds of them, waiting right outside the door. As the soldiers pushed the outer doors open, Jesus was swallowed by the multitude.

CHAPTER 35

We go live to David Hiller, our Middle East correspondent in Tel Aviv," Barr announced from the anchor's desk as the image on the studio monitor shifted. Hiller was having a terrible time just staying in front of the camera as he yelled over the tumult.

"Andrew, I have been following this story from the beginning and it gets more incredible all the time." He suddenly ducked to escape a projectile being hurled over his head at Jesus. He got closer to the camera.

"Apparently, the military commanders have decided that the case is too emotional an issue for them to handle. Authorities are convinced that this man is a fraud, but also fear a large fringe element who prefer to see him as some kind of prophet. There is still no proof connecting him to the Jerusalem bomb in any way, but authorities do not rule out the possibility that he may somehow be implicated. With all the evidence having been destroyed in Beirut, there is no way to connect him to that bombing either."

"David, isn't it possible he may be able to identify the real perpetrators?" Barr questioned from the studio. "And if so, why let him go?"

"I think the military is hoping the media will work for them, rather than against them for a change, to expose this man as a fraud and get what information they can."

Hiller was in the same quandary as the rest of the world, and his voice reflected his feelings. At this moment he seemed less the hard core journalist, and more like a real human being.

"Military leaders don't feel an aggressive stance would be popular under the circumstances," he continued. "They reason that with the amount of coverage the story's received, there is no way for this man to disappear, and if he slips and exposes any accomplices, he will hopefully do it on television for all the world to witness."

Barr broke in from the studio. "David, I'm still confused as to why this man is being given any credence at all? There have always been people who claimed they were Jesus. Why has this man attracted so much attention?"

"It's a combination of things, Andrew. He attracted attention at a time when the world was in a state of despair. There were many people who were looking for some ray of good to come out of all of this. Sitting outside that building, in a city that experts say should not be standing today, a city with more emotional ties throughout the world than any other perhaps, convinced a lot of people that his claims were genuine. So far there is no evidence against him; he has no identification, indeed no money. Most importantly are the wounds that his doctors reported, wounds that coincide with those which Jesus would have suffered, wounds which the military claims were purposely inflicted as part of an overall sting operation, a sting operation which at this moment seems to have been perfectly thought out and executed."

"A fascinating story, thank-you for that report, David. An interesting situation which we will follow closely." Barr switched to a new camera. "Elsewhere in the news, Pakistan and India renewed threats of nuclear retaliation today…"

Jesus was surrounded by a veritable sea of flesh; reporters, photographers, people trying to touch him, others throwing objects, screaming, cursing. The colonel had been correct in his assessment, and Jesus was beginning to wonder if he would come through this in one piece.

"Please, let me through. Please!" He shouted, but to no avail, the crowd was on a rampage. Instead he was propelled forward in a direction not of his own choosing.

"Please," he shouted again, "why are you doing this?"

"Save me, Jesus!" The voice of an old man came from the crowd. "Please, save me!"

"Fraud. You son-of-a-bitch!" an angry voice screamed from another direction. Jesus turned his head, but could not tell who had spoken amongst the sea of faces.

"Someone ought to shoot you!" a woman standing next to him yelled, reaching out and punching his side as hard as she could. He winced in pain.

A white limousine was slowly making its way through the crowd toward Jesus. No sooner did it come to a stop when the crowd slammed Jesus onto the hood. Two of the limo doors forced their way open and a middle-aged man dressed in a white suit, as well as two body guards, stepped into the crowd, trying to get to Jesus.

"My name is Carter Eban," the man in white shouted over the noise. "Please, get into the car."

"I don't understand," Jesus yelled back, trying to extricate himself from the ravaging mass.

"You won't last much longer in this," Eban begged. "Let me help you." "I don't know you." Jesus was at a loss. Should he trust this man? Did he have a choice?

Eban could see the confusion on his face. "Look, you've got to trust someone. Please, get in the car, let me help you. At least I can offer you a little peace and quiet."

Someone from behind slammed Jesus back against the vehicle. Eban's bodyguards pushed the crowd back slightly. Eban waited for a moment, then turned and moved toward the car door. After taking a quick glance around, Jesus followed with the guards running interference. Jesus escaped the hands that were on him and got into the car. The door immediately slammed behind him.

"Bulletproof," Eban quipped, as his hand reached out and hit the locks. "Even the Pope has to have one these days."

Much of the noise seemed to disappear, save an occasional hand hitting the roof or window. The car was easing forward, and with the push of another button, window screens came down, blocking the outside view. After a few tense moments, the driver urged the limo out of the crowd.

Jesus breathed a sigh of relief. A trickle of blood flowed from his forehead where he had been hit by flying debris. Eban offered him a handkerchief.

"Who are you?" Jesus asked, taking the cloth, studying the man's face. "As I said, my name is Carter Eban. Please. Relax. We shouldn't be very long."

Jesus decided to take the man's advice. He settled back into the luxurious seat, too tired to talk at the moment.

CHAPTER 36

The driver had done a good job evading the few reporters who managed to get to their vehicles and give chase. No one had seemed prepared for the turn of events, and hampered by the size of the crowd, the media overall was slow to pursue.

They drove for a considerable amount of time before Eban's limo pulled up to his huge estate. Eban had raised the window screens so Jesus could see outside. A guardhouse stood next to a formidable sliding gate. Behind the fence, trained dogs protected the premise with ferocity. A helicopter hovered overhead. They stopped for only a moment. As soon as the guards confirmed it was indeed Eban, the gates opened.

They drove for several minutes through beautifully manicured gardens and swaying palms before pulling up to the mansion itself. A doorman helped Jesus from the car.

Eban got out on his own and walked toward the entrance. He stopped halfway up the steps and turned back. Jesus was looking around the grounds; tennis courts, pools, gardens, waterfalls, all set against the backdrop of the Mediterranean. He had never seen anything like it.

"Right this way." Eban smiled. "You must not be shy. I want you to feel at home."

Jesus followed him inside.

After viewing the outside, it would have been difficult to believe that the inside would be even more impressive, but it was. Every appointment had been specially selected, from the exquisite furniture, to the original paintings on the walls, the sculptures in the corners, the marble floors covered with the finest Persian rugs, Arabic style stone carved arches and mosaic tiles. It was clear that no expense had been spared.

An atrium, equipped with sliding glass doors stretched along the entire backside of the mansion, allowing for a panoramic view of the sea. There was an interior waterfall and pond, the sound of which, coupled with the chirping of flitting birds, provided a wonderful, soothing ambiance.

Jesus stood in the middle of the atrium, trying to take everything in. He was stunned by the beauty, the aroma, and lavishness of it all. Eban opened his arms congenially.

"Welcome to my humble abode."

Jesus said nothing, and after a moment, Eban dropped his arms. He surmised what Jesus was feeling, and felt ashamed.

"You know, the gates won't keep them out forever, but it will take awhile before they track you down. Meanwhile, my home is yours."

"You are very kind," Jesus said graciously, finding himself at a loss for words.

"Thank-you, but you are entirely wrong," Eban corrected with a smile. "I can, however, recognize a kind individual when I meet one. You see, there are so few in this world."

"Perhaps you don't know where to look," Jesus responded.

Eban smiled at the comment, then walked over to the bell pull on the wall and rang for an attendant.

"This is all yours?" Jesus asked, looking out at the blue sea.

"This one, and several others quite like it. In other parts of the world of course."

A man entered the room dressed in a white uniform. He was an older gentleman with a kindly face.

"Yes, sir? You called?" the servant said humbly.

Eban smiled at the man and spoke respectfully. "Yes. Bring our guest some refreshment. Food and something to drink." He turned to Jesus. "Do you have a preference?"

Jesus shook his head. "Whatever you have is fine."

"Very well, sir." The servant bowed and departed.

"I know how terrible hospital food can be," Eban said with a grin. "You look tired."

"The last few days have been quite an ordeal."

"After you eat, my servant will show you to your room so you can rest." He smiled, and stood up as if to leave.

Jesus sensed that Eban was uncomfortable around him, and simultaneously drawn to him. It was obvious that Eban was a complex man, but what was driving him to do this evaded Jesus entirely.

"Why does a man with so many servants come to my rescue?"

Eban hesitated for a moment before he spoke. "Because I believe you are who some say you are." Jesus looked surprised, but said nothing. "The authorities are too terrified to consider it. They may lose what little control they have. I, on the other hand, have nothing to fear." He came over to Jesus and looked directly into his eyes. "Your presence at the sight of that unexploded bomb was surely a miracle."

"Life is the only miracle. So many have lost theirs. Such a needless waste."

"But they were just little people."

Jesus found the callousness of Eban's statement appalling. He drew a sharp breath, but Eban stopped him with raised hand: "I apologize. I don't mean to sound brutal, but it's true. You, on the other hand, are very significant to the scheme of things. The world is in an intolerable mess. No one wants it that way, but we are stuck with it nonetheless. Perhaps you can offer a way out."

"My answers are the same as they always were," Jesus responded testily.

"Yes." Eban smiled.

The attendant returned with a tray of assorted breads, meats, and fruits, as well as a pitcher of fresh juice. He set it on a table in front of a divan and motioned for Jesus to sit.

"Thank-you," Jesus said, moving toward the food.

"You are most welcome, sir." The attendant bowed and disappeared.

Jesus sat and found himself admiring the tray. It had been meticulously prepared. The fruits were perfectly ripened and full of color, cut into assorted shapes; diamonds, stars, wedges, and rounds. There was a small vase of fresh cut flowers in the center, and the pitcher was of the finest cut glass, even a finger bowl and towel.

"How does one acquire such opulence? Are you royalty?"

"Quite the contrary. I inhabit the bottom of the pit."

The answer confused Jesus further. He studied Eban, frustrated that he could not put the pieces together for himself. Finally Eban completed the puzzle for him.

"I am an arms dealer. I sell weapons."

Jesus set the piece of fruit he had selected back on the tray without taking a bite. He wiped his fingers with the towel.

"To whom?" Jesus asked guardedly.

"To anyone who would buy them." Eban confessed.

Jesus' mind raced. He looked around the room. Had he misunderstood? Could a society actually condone the acquisition of wealth through such an enterprise?

"You bought this by selling guns?" Jesus asked incredulously.

"Guns, tanks, ships, jets, bombs, mortars. Anything that was needed."

"Needed!"

"Yes." Eban bowed his head, his voice apologetic.

"Why?" Jesus exclaimed.

"Because people wanted them and were willing to pay."

"You have lived off the misery of others!"

"As you can see, I had no shortage of customers." Eban could see the anger in Jesus' eyes, and heard the void in his own statement. "I had always told myself that I was performing a valuable function, one that others would fill if I didn't. I convinced myself that I was helping to maintain the balance of power for all the little countries who bought my wares."

"If they had no weapons to fight with, wouldn't the power still be balanced?"

"Yes, I finally made the same observation myself," Eban responded sadly. "By that time I was quite rich." He took a deep breath. "That is why I picked you up today. I viewed it as a token step toward repaying my debt to the world, though I know it won't keep me from the fires of Hell."

"How does one reconcile being a dealer of death?"

Eban absorbed the admonishment graciously. "Your world is too simple. It doesn't reflect reality. The changes occur slowly, year after year, decade after decade, death upon death. Wrong becomes right, and right, wrong. One is born and raised in the existing circumstances, and hatred is perpetuated by the fathers. Revenge replaces all other religions, and it is the most personal of all."

Jesus rose from the couch and moved toward the atrium windows, searching within himself for answers. "How arrogant I am. To have thought that my living might have really made a difference."

"Not at all. Just think of how bad things would have been without you."

"They could hardly be worse."

"On the contrary, the fact that you are here is proof of hope. I don't know how you got here, nor how you learned the things you know, but your appearance is no doubt significant. You see, somewhere deep inside, even the worst of us understand the inherent goodness of the human soul, and hope it will triumph in the end."

Jesus didn't say a word for several seconds. He then turned to Eban and said bluntly: "I must go."

This change in attitude took Eban quite by surprise. He had been prepared for many possible reactions, however, not this one. "But you just got here. You need to rest."

"I am grateful for your hospitality, but I cannot accept it," Jesus replied, moving toward the door.

"You don't forgive me."

"Sometimes forgiveness is hard to find." Jesus stopped and turned to Eban. "Give away your wealth. Help those whose suffering have given you so much. In that way may you find your salvation."

"I can't do that. It's not that simple." Eban's voice was filled with remorse.

"But it is."

"At least take this," Eban said, reaching into his pocket and taking out money. "You'll need it."

"I have no need of your money," Jesus responded angrily.

"Please, you don't understand!" Eban pleaded. "In this matter you must trust me. It is necessary. Use it as a tool to do what you must do. It has little importance to me. Its value is illusionary."

"Then what purpose will it serve? Why will you not give it away?"

"You can give it purpose."

"First, you must show me how." Jesus opened the door.

"I will tell the guards to open the gate for you," Eban said, giving in.

Jesus stood in the doorway, his back to Eban. "Were you responsible for the destruction of Beirut? For the bomb in Jerusalem?"

Eban was moved to tears. "No. I have never dealt in nuclear weapons."

Jesus paused for a moment, but never looked back. "Do what I say. Your disease is cured."

Eban dropped to his knees. No one but his doctors knew of the illness from which he was suffering. "How did you know?" he yelled.

Jesus did not respond as he kept walking toward the front gate.

CHAPTER 37

As he moved down the long drive, Jesus was overcome by a crushing sense of failure. Not only had his words been wasted on deaf ears, his very existence had become a source of conflict? The world was still in turmoil, people still suffered, wars were still being fought, only now in some cases it was done in his name.

At the front gates the guards let him through without question. Eban had kept his word. Jesus began walking down the road, but had no idea where he was going. Nothing looked familiar, but at least he was alone. The solitude, however, was short-lived, as a windblown man in khakis came running up from behind.

"Mind if I tag along?" David Hiller asked as he drew even with Jesus.

"You are free to walk where you like," Jesus said without stopping. "How did you find me?"

Hiller laughed, pulling a hand out of one pocket and pointing toward the Mediterranean, a chopper hovering above the water. "Just followed the helicopter that followed you. That's still following you," Hiller corrected. "The rest of the vultures will be right along. Count on it."

Jesus kept walking at a good clip without making any response.

"Cozying up with an ex-arms dealer is not going to sit well with the general public you know? Bad for the image. It's the first mistake your little masquerade has made." Hiller hoped a little guilt would get him the intended reaction. He wasn't disappointed.

Jesus suddenly stopped walking and turned toward the audacious reporter. He had never hit anyone in his life, having come close only once, but now he found himself teetering on the edge. "I did not know who he was. He rescued me from an impossible situation. Besides, people change." He began walking again.

"Not guys like him," Hiller said, catching up. "Look, my Rover's right back there. Let me give you a ride."

"I don't think so."

"In a couple of minutes this place is going to be swarming, just like the hospital."

Jesus slowed. Then stopped. "There's no escape?"

"Just me," Hiller said lightly. He gave Jesus a moment to digest the situation. "Come on." He started walking away, motioning toward the vehicle with his head, his hands still casually in his pockets.

Jesus thought for a moment, then followed.

"Who are you?" Jesus asked as they drove back toward Tel Aviv. The man was brash, but Jesus found himself strangely drawn to him. While Jesus wasn't sure he could trust him, he believed Hiller to be telling the truth.

"My name is David Hiller. I work for a major U.S. network. I've been following you from the start, when they discovered you and the bomb in Jerusalem. Quite frankly, I couldn't believe what I was hearing. What's the real story?"

"I don't know," Jesus said over the sound of the wind and a passing car.

"Come on," Hiller insisted genially. "You're a free man." His tone became a little more serious. "They've thrown you to the wolves. At least this one will try to get you a fair trial."

"Are all people today as skeptical as you?"

"Of course," Hiller stated with a laugh. "You saw what happened. Over half a mil lost their lives. Hardly leaves room for much optimism. People are scared. They figure these guys won't stop till it's all over."

"These guys?"

"The terrorists. Who'd you think I meant?"

"What do you want from me?"

"An exclusive interview for my network." This was feeling far too easy Hiller thought to himself. Was he really thinking of taking the bait? David fought to control his zeal. But he was so close! If he could snag this one, his career would be set for life. "I get you on television, and you talk. Simple as that. Tell us who you are, and who you work for."

"I have never found it advantageous to overly publicize myself. It invariably leads to trouble."

Hiller looked at Jesus and laughed. "A sense of humor. I like that. Of course, you're already a little late on the overly publicized part."

Jesus thought for a moment. He was starting to understand the game and how it was played. "Tell me, what do I get in return?"

"Now your talking!" Hiller's voice was enthusiastic. "How much would you settle for?"

"I want a ride. To Jerusalem."

Hiller stopped the car. "You're kidding?"

"No. I'm quite serious." Jesus had thought his request fairly reasonable.

"That's all? Transportation?"

"That's all."

Hiller started laughing uproariously as he slapped the steering wheel. "You got it. When do you want to do it?"

"The sooner the better," Jesus said, not wanting to wait.

"I'll take you right to the station."

CHAPTER 38

The television studio in Tel Aviv was buzzing. Technicians were refocusing lights, setting furniture, checking sound levels, and moving cameras into position. Jesus stood to the side watching. Before long David Hiller and a makeup person approached him, obviously in a hurry.

Hiller glanced at his watch. "Getting close. Any objection to wearing a little makeup? You'll show up better on camera."

"I prefer not…"

Hiller hadn't even listened. He looked at the technician, "Go ahead and slap a little on him."

The technician began giving Jesus a little color, and applying powder.

"Now this will be a live interview, so don't freeze up in front of the camera." Hiller glanced around a little nervously. "The anchor in New York is a reporter named Andrew Barr. I've worked with him for a long time and he's usually pretty fair." He lit a cigarette. "Now, when the camera's red light is lit, it means you're on. You'll be able to see Andy in the monitor directly over the camera." He pointed to the apparatus as he spoke. "Now, there may be a slight delay in the signals, but I don't think it'll throw you. Any questions?" he asked, rubbing his hands together.

"Will I be able to say anything I want?"

"He'll expect you to answer his questions, but there's always room for editorial comment," Hiller smiled slyly. "There are, of course, the usual time restraints, no cussing, and so on. Oh, and there'll be several breaks for commercials."

"Of course," Jesus said with a touch of cynicism.

By this time the tech had finished with the makeup. The floor director called out the time.

"We've got sixty seconds till air."

"Sounds like they're ready to start," Hiller said, straightening Jesus' robe. "We better get you into place."

He led Jesus to the chair in front of the camera and clipped a small microphone to his clothing.

"Thirty seconds," the floor director called out.

"Here's a pitcher of water if you get thirsty." Hiller poured the first glass.

"Ten seconds."

"Good luck," Hiller said, patting Jesus on the shoulder. "I'll bet there'll be an easy two billion people watching you." He turned and left Jesus sitting alone.

Andrew Barr had done many interviews in his life, but nothing could compare to this—interviewing Jesus Christ! It was definitely something he had never envisioned himself doing. Did he believe it? Probably not. But he had to admit he had some lingering doubts. He had seen enough of the man on clips to realize that there was something different about him. He had also concluded for himself that the man had not been implicated in the bombing of Beirut. He had nothing scientific to base the decision on, it was strictly instinct. And then there was the failed attempt to blow up Jerusalem. The miracle.

Above all, Andrew felt presumptuous. Presumptuous for even taking the interview seriously, as it would surely offend the memory of the real Jesus. On the other hand, it would be presumptuous to not take the interview seriously, just in case it was the real Jesus. After all, wasn't that what happened to Jesus in Jerusalem in the first place? It was a no win situation, and Barr was not sure how he would handle it. Plenty of people offered advice, of course. But he would be the one on the spot, asking the questions. He finally relaxed and decided to take it one step at a time.

The television monitor Jesus was looking at came to life with Andrew Barr seated behind the news desk in New York. Flashy music played as a female announcer did an introductory voice over.

"'USA A.M.', America's number one morning magazine brings you this live, special, news-maker interview. We go live to GBC news correspondent, Andrew Barr."

Jesus' heart began to race. Two billion people! The number was staggering. The reality of what was happening was just beginning to sink in. He thought of his friends on board Resurrection, and wished they could be here with him.

"Good morning," Barr said to the viewing audience. "More than two weeks have passed since the world breathed a collective sigh of relief for Jerusalem, and the Middle East. Today, GBC news correspondent, David Hiller, has managed to arrange an exclusive interview with the man who was found outside the building where that bomb was discovered. The man who calls himself, Jesus. We go directly to Tel Aviv."

The red light on top of the camera illuminated, and Andrew Barr was suddenly speaking directly to Jesus.

"Though it is evening in Tel Aviv, it is early morning for our viewers. Welcome, and thank-you for the opportunity to talk with you." Barr's voice was steady and cordial. Jesus felt a small bit of relief.

"You are welcome."

"You claim your name is Jesus, is that correct?" Barr had decided to get this major issue out of the way first.

Jesus knew this question was fraught with dangers. He wanted to be sincere, and believed. At the same time he understood that much of his story would sound preposterous, even to a society awash in science fiction and fantasy. "Is my name so important?" he answered elusively, yet knowing it would not be enough.

"I think our viewers would be interested in the truth." Barr would not allow it. To him the issue was fundamental, and critical. What could the real Jesus possibly have to hide?

"Yes. My name is Jesus," he said, finally giving in. He realized there was no turning back now.

"And your last name?"

As the interview went forward, another audience, not far from where the Tel Aviv studio was located, listened with extreme interest. The three terrorists were readying their weapons, and gathering their things. Opportunity had knocked, and the plan had come together quickly. On the surface it seemed relatively simple. They knew where Jesus was, and when he came out of the studio after the interview, they would be waiting. Once they had him, they were confident their safety would be assured.

Dace picked up his Uzi, then turned to Kobra and Basel. "Let's go."

"I was born in Bethlehem," Jesus said, answering Barr's question. "I am a Nazarene, a descendant from the House of David. And though I know that is hard to believe, it is true."

Whatever Barr might have been thinking, his face showed no visible sign. He was a consummate professional, and responded to Jesus thoughtfully. "In that case, I will simply address you as Jesus, is that all right?"

"Yes."

Barr picked his way forward carefully. It was a unique situation, and he was determined to do away with the normal slick interview, promising himself that he would take his time. Whoever this man was, he would try to be fair.

"As you are probably aware, world attention was focused on you after you were discovered outside the building with the bomb. Experts are still in a quandary as to why it didn't explode. Can you offer us an explanation?"

"As I have told all who have asked me this question, I have no answer—except for prayer."

Jesus looked at Barr on the studio monitor. The answer was so simple and straight forward, the expression on his face so benign, that Barr found himself caught off guard.

"How is it that you happened to be in Jerusalem?"

"Palestine is my home. Is it so unusual for a Jew to be there?"

"How did you know where the bomb was?"

His questions were relentless, and Jesus was feeling trapped. "I just knew."

"I see." Barr sensed he had found a chink in his armor, but how to proceed? He gathered his thoughts and regrouped. The interview was starting to remind him of some chess matches he had been involved with in college. He moved to the next question, he would come back to this one later.

"The doctors in Tel Aviv reported several wounds which have been highly publicized, wounds which they claim bear a striking resemblance to those which would have been suffered by victims of a crucifixion, an ancient form of execution. Is that correct?"

"It is true that I bear these scars, yes."

"Were you indeed crucified?"

"Yes."

"Do you claim to be the same Jesus who was crucified nearly two thousand years ago by Pontius Pilate?"

"Yes. I am that same person."

Barr could feel his adrenaline rushing. He knew he was definitely in no man's land. "What proof can you offer the world?"

"None."

Barr felt a surge of disappointment with that answer. It had changed everything. After all the hype, he had no proof! But why was Barr feeling such anger? He'd never really believed the story in the first place. Or was he harboring a hope that even he wasn't aware of? He fought to get his questions back on track.

"Yet you insist that you are the person that all Christians recognize as their Savior?"

"I am. And am not."

Great segue, Barr thought.

As Jesus prepared to explain, much to his surprise, Barr changed the subject completely. It had the effect of a glass of ice water being thrown at his face.

"And we will pick it up right there when we come back," Barr said, as the network broke for a commercial.

Mance hovered in back of Volk as they watched the broadcast. They were probably as nervous as Jesus was, but for different reasons.

"We've got him isolated. We know exactly where he is," Volk said, turning to Mance. "I think this may be our best opportunity."

Mance reflected on the situation, which still had a thousand possible pitfalls. His head moved nervously up and down, then finally: "Call Kaseel. Tell him to get the locator ready."

The commercial break had ended and Barr was back on the air.

"Now, returning to our guest. I asked you if you were the man whom Christians claim as their Savior?"

Jesus had been sitting there for two minutes, trying to compose his thoughts, yet now that the camera was on, everything he had meant to say seemed to fly out of his brain. Commercial television made inspiration very difficult.

"Yes," he answered, finally regaining his sense of where they had left off. "However, though I am that same person, I do not recognize myself as the savior of mankind."

"Why?" Barr inquired, intrigued by the response.

"Because I failed."

Barr froze. His image flashed on the screen momentarily. No doubt the board operator noted the perplexed look on his face. It wasn't often that a news anchor let his true feelings slip out over the air.

During Barr's lapse, Jesus continued. "Mankind, for all his technological advances, has not changed appreciably since the time of the Romans. What has changed is that people now use my name to justify their behavior. Many who call themselves Christians will reject me, since to accept who I am, is to accept my shame."

This was dangerous territory, and Barr knew it. There was little doubt in his mind that the majority of his viewing audience would be deeply offended, and he could already feel a trickle of sweat rolling down his back. While he knew he was no biblical scholar, it was up to him to ask the tough questions, to address their concerns, and to corner this man, whosoever he might be.

"Jesus, correct me if I'm wrong, but I always understood that the salvation you offered mankind was eternal life for those who accepted you as their Savior. Yet you seem to equate salvation with saving the planet and the people on it in a more material sense. I'm confused. Can you straighten me out on this point?" Barr felt confident he had him trapped.

"Eternal life is dependent upon acts in the present. So much concern is given to what will come, while what *is* begs for change. Is not what I am tomorrow, dependent on what I do today?"

He was cagey, and Barr felt him squirming free. He switched the line of questioning.

"Jerusalem is the center for three of the world's great religions. When we come back, I would like you to answer, in your view, which of those religions has the greatest claim to that city? We will be back in a moment."

As soon as he knew the connection was broken for the commercial break, Barr looked at the floor director. "Slippery. Very slippery." The director nodded.

As news of the television broadcast spread, reporters began gathering at the studio entrance. This time, however, there was less bedlam. Instead, the majority of the reporters listened to the interview over their own equipment—many were moved by the common sense words they were hearing. The message was simple, which is what they thought it was supposed to be from the very beginning.

A block away, the terrorists sat in their car, watching the entrance nervously. They had not considered the reporters' presence, but it was too late to alter their plans now. They would just have to deal with the situation as it developed, and reporters were expendable.

Kobra sat in the front passenger seat. She lit a cigarette, then looked at her watch. Basel was behind the wheel. He checked his rear view. So far all was quiet. He turned his attention back to the studio entrance.

Jesus was gaining in confidence. During this last commercial break he had decided he needed to take matters into his own hands or he would never say what he felt he needed to. As the interview picked up he took the lead, cutting Barr off mid-sentence.

"You were asking me who had the greater claim."

"In your view, yes," Barr responded, letting the forwardness slide. "Who's right, and who's wrong?"

"It's not a matter of right and wrong. It has to do with love and hate. As long as there is hatred, there will be those who exploit it."

"But wouldn't you concur that in this instance, everyone has been right and wrong to varying degrees?

"There are no degrees in killing," Jesus stated resolutely. "If you kill one person needlessly, while I kill sixty, does that make you more right than I am? No. It's merely justification for more killing. The first step to restoring world peace is to stop the killing. Universally! Every person taking responsibility for their actions, searching out all the hidden ways man kills his kind. I would rather die than take a life, no matter the reason."

"Those are fine sentiments," Barr came back, "but they are a bit simplistic, don't you think?"

Simplistic? Perhaps. Yet for all its simplicity mankind has not even come close to accomplishing it."

"Yes," Barr interrupted, "but there always have been, and always will be a few sick individuals in any society. Troublemakers who must be controlled."

"If only it were just a few troublemakers. Unfortunately in some cases it is entire nations, religions, races, cultures, all the individuals contained therein, all justifying their revenge. But when will there be enough revenge for peace? If not today, then perhaps tomorrow? How about next week? Or next year?" Jesus paused, searching for the right words. "Grace towards others is easy in simple, everyday matters. But it is in matters of killing and hate where absolution is most difficult. It tests our faith, and demands courage, strength, and obedience to find forgiveness, especially when we feel none. So, tell me, when is a good time for the killing to stop?

He waited for an answer, but Barr never replied.

"The present is the only time, and therein lies the world's salvation. Governments, religions, and all individuals must all recognize that any policy that takes lives is doomed to fail!"

"I'm sure that many political and religious leaders would disagree with you," Barr admonished.

"It would not be the first time. My ideas were always considered somewhat dangerous." Jesus paused a moment to gauge Barr's reaction. "There are many ways to live and enjoy life, but all ways must adhere to the concepts of love and goodness. Love is life's constant, the yardstick for living."

"Are you implying that your way is the only way?"

"God's way! God's commandments are a guide to life. The principles are inherent in the teachings of all the great religions because we all share the same God. Any man who adheres to them shall find eternal salvation, no matter what his religious preference. A man should not require the promise of eternal life or the threat of damnation to be good. If he does, he has missed the point altogether. If that is all his religions have given him, then they should be thrown out and forgotten! Men know in their hearts what is right, and what is wrong. In truth they have no need to be told."

Barr could almost hear an audible gasp from around the world. He wondered how the ratings were looking.

"That's a very strong condemnation. I'm not sure our viewers can accept your words are those of Jesus Christ."

"Those that cannot, have chosen to make the teachings conform to their lives, rather than conforming their lives to the teachings. While some may denounce me, the world waits for the Savior to return. But how will it recognize him? How will he possibly fit into your world? You have isolated yourselves. You profess to want change while you convince yourselves it is not possible. But it is, if people are willing to give, to share the burden of suffering, to care about more than who is right and who is wrong. To forgive. Don't you see? The message is more important than the man. The Savior can be anyone who can find a way to make the world listen, and change. I only hope that person comes before it's too late."

"And we will return right after this message."

CHAPTER 39

The studio control room in New York City looked almost like its counterpart aboard Resurrection, filled with monitors and technicians with headsets. Toward the back of the room, a number of men, station execs, were huddled together, commiserating, a burst of raucous laughter erupting every few seconds. The door behind them opened and a woman rushed in, papers in hand, and joined them. She barely had breath enough to speak.

"The calls are coming in fast and furious. We've never had this kind of response," she said, gulping for air.

"Good or bad?" one of the men asked.

"Both. And both in the extreme." She leafed through some of the papers she carried. "Some people are convinced he is the real Jesus, others are so incensed they think he should be jailed, or shot." She handed him an example. "I can tell you this, few of the religious leaders are responding positively. Most think this is all in the poorest of taste." Her tone became extremely solemn. "They're angry that we're even broadcasting it."

"Too late!" one of the execs shouted in delight. "I guess our ratings'll have to just go through the roof!"

One of the men was watching the monitor, listening to the conversation behind him with only half an ear. Somewhere inside him, Jesus had connected, but he was very apprehensive to say so. "Does anyone here believe this guy?"

"Come on, get serious," one of the others responded, sounding truly irritated. "Just because the guy is news doesn't mean he's real."

"But you can't deny there's a simple truth to what he says," the woman suggested. "If Jesus were to come today, I could believe it would be him."

"I could tell you the simple truth too, but it wouldn't change anything!" The room ignited into a new round of laughter as the cynical exec moved toward the door, milking the situation for all it was worth. "Get me out of here, before I'm born again."

CHAPTER 40

The interview had ended and Jesus felt shaky. The questions had been difficult, and it was hard to be honest, while not disclosing the existence of the aliens, as if anyone would have believed him in the first place. He grabbed the chair's armrest and stood just as David Hiller got to him.

"God, that was great!" Hiller said as he helped Jesus remove the microphone. "You made me a rich man today."

"At least some benefit was derived." Jesus' head was still swimming.

"The report from the States is a lot of people are really buying your story." Hiller's enthusiasm was childlike, but it was all just a game to him.

"You don't?"

"Not really." Hiller raised his eyebrows as if to say, are you kidding? Then he patted Jesus on the back. "But I plan to keep my end of the bargain, although why you even want to get near Jerusalem now is beyond me. We'll leave as soon as you can get your things together."

Jesus touched his robe. "I have everything I need with me. We can go now if you wish."

"Sure, fine with me. Let me just tell them when I'll be back. There's a Chicago pizza joint down on the waterfront. We'll grab a bite to eat there before we head out. My treat. It's the least I can do for you."

Hiller rushed off across the studio floor.

To the outsider, Jerusalem might have seemed normal again. But to those who had always lived there, something was different. The majority had moved back into the ancient city. Shops had reopened, as well as hospitals, restaurants, and most everything else. In some ways things seemed almost more cordial, rather than less.

Everyone knew the bomb had been found, and most assumed that the perpetrators would eventually be caught since the government had hard evidence in the unexploded bomb. But whatever small amount of tranquility the city had previously enjoyed, was totally shattered. The terrorists had stepped over the line with Beirut, and there was a sense that eventually, since the seed had been planted, someone would try again with Jerusalem.

History. It was what everyone who lived there loved, and hated, about Jerusalem. And Jesus was going back.

The studio entrance had slowly turned into a zoo, packed with double the reporters and vehicles. The atmosphere had remained friendly enough with people milling about; waiting, chatting, drinking coffee and soda. But once the broadcast had reached its conclusion, everyone started jockeying for position. They were all in place now, and they knew it wouldn't be long.

As the terrorists watched, their level of anxiety started to build. They pulled their weapons from the back seat and checked their clips one last time, keeping the guns below the level of the dash to avoid picking up any flashes of light. Dace flipped his cigarette out onto the street. Basel couldn't wait.

As soon as the studio door opened the entire atmosphere changed. The reporters switched personalities like trained attack dogs, and Jesus and David Hiller were assaulted by a barrage of questions fired at them from every side. They made their way down the stairs, inching toward Hiller's vehicle, pushed and pulled the entire time.

It was hard to be certain, but Jesus thought he noticed a familiar figure in the crowd, moving in his direction. At first he dismissed the idea, for he knew no one in this time period. His curiosity got the better of him though, and when he looked back a second time, the figure seemed to be returning his gaze. Then it dawned on him.

It was Kaseel, cloaked, his delicate frame pushing its way through the crowd. Jesus turned and started to move toward him.

"Where are you going?" Hiller shouted, grabbing his arm.

"There's something I have to do."

"You're crazy! We've got to get out of here!"

The delay had been just long enough for Kaseel to make his way over. As soon as he was next to Jesus, Kaseel grabbed his arm.

"This will hurt only a little."

Kaseel smiled, and before Jesus had a chance to respond, injected the tiny locator. Then, almost as quickly as they had met, the crowd separated them, their eyes retaining contact for a few seconds beyond.

Hiller had sensed something odd about the transaction, but there was no time to ask questions now. He grabbed Jesus abruptly and started pulling him toward his vehicle. "Come on!"

It was at that moment that the terrorists made their move. The car slammed into gear and raced forward up the street, coming to a screeching halt directly in front of the studio entrance. Everything stopped for a moment as the crowd seemed to sense that something was about to happen, but had no idea what that was.

Then the doors of the car swung open and three people jumped out, striking in a sudden explosion of violence. Machine gun fire ripped through the bewildered crowd. Many went down immediately, others panicked and tried to run, only to be cut down in flight. Most, however, simply fell to the ground, their hands over their heads, praying for the nightmare to end.

David Hiller was one of those who was sprawled on the ground, his instincts honed by the experience of war. He looked up and saw Jesus standing, facing the gunmen. Hiller was about to cry out when the firing stopped and one of the terrorists addressed the crowd.

"Everyone on the ground or you will die!" Dace was waving the Uzi around wildly.

Many people were screaming, crying, but all obeyed without question.

It was at that moment that Jesus turned and saw Kaseel still standing, with no one between them.

"Kaseel! Lie down!" Jesus yelled, motioning him to the ground. But Kaseel seemed frozen with fear. Jesus ran toward him, calling at the top of his lungs, "Lie down!"

But before Kaseel had a chance to respond, Jesus heard the sound of machine guns. Kaseel's body convulsed until the firing stopped, then he fell to the ground, his body riddled with bullets.

"No!" Jesus wailed, dropping to the alien's side and gathering him in his arms.

Kobra rushed to Jesus and stuck the muzzle of her weapon against the back of his head.

"Get in the car!"

Jesus cradled Kaseel's fragile body. There was no sign of life. He rocked him gently back and forth.

"Get in the car, Jew!" the woman screamed.

Jesus stroked Kaseel's face, ignoring her threats. "Why?" he asked mournfully.

Dace and Basel came up from behind and grabbed Jesus, wrenching him toward their vehicle. Dace screamed at Jesus, and waved his weapon toward the crowd.

"Get into the car now, or all these people will die!"

He shot one person to prove his threat was real, then fired several more bursts into the air. Without hesitation, Jesus turned and got into the car. Before the doors even closed, the vehicle sped down the street.

The instant the three terrorists pulled away, David Hiller leapt to his feet and raced for his vehicle. His good fortune had turned into a nightmare. While he might not have believed the stranger's story, he seemed a decent human being, and this was hardly what Hiller had envisioned for him. And the mystery surrounding the being who had been shot after touching Jesus was also unsettling.

Hiller wished he had other options as he started the engine, but he knew he didn't. He was the man's only hope at this point. As he headed after the fast disappearing car, he unholstered his cell phone and threw it on the seat.

The door to the studio opened slowly until those inside could confirm the coast was clear. Once they realized it was safe, they stepped outside and saw the carnage. One person screamed, and several others sobbed. The rest moved quickly to help the injured.

One man tried to get to his feet. He rose halfway, then stumbled back, bleeding profusely. One of the studio technicians, a woman, ran to him, catching him just as he hit the ground. She saw the terror in his eyes. "Oh my God," she whispered to herself. In a moment, the man was gone.

The terrorists' car careened through the city streets at perilous speed. They had carried off the abduction, but how the rest of the scenario would play out they could only guess. The element of surprise had been with them, and as far as they could tell, no one was following. But they also knew the Israeli Army, and they knew they would be waiting for them.

Dace sat with Jesus in the back seat, the gun pointed at Jesus' head a constant reminder of the precarious situation he was in. Still, as was typical, Jesus thought not about himself, but of Kaseel, and his sacrifice.

"Why? Why did you do that? What was gained?" Jesus yelled at his captives.

Dace viciously poked Jesus' head with the barrel of his weapon. "Shut up, Jew. You'll find out what it is to pay for the sins of your people soon enough!"

"There is someone following us!" Basel warned, glancing into his rear view mirror.

Dace pulled his gun off of Jesus and held it out the window, firing multiple bursts at the approaching vehicle.

Instinctively, Jesus pulled on the terrorist's arm. "No!"

He hadn't even realized it was coming. A smashing blow to his head from behind knocked him to the floor of the car. Dace shoved the gun back out the window and resumed firing.

There was nothing Jesus could do in his half-conscious state. He remained semi-lucid for only a moment, then slipped into unconsciousness. The woman spit as she lifted her weapon back over the front seat and turned forward. She looked at Basel and said only one thing: "Go faster!"

Hiller was weaving back and forth in an effort to dodge the storm of bullets that were ricocheting off his vehicle. He thought about the sports car he had almost bought last year, and how useful it would have been under the circumstances. Then he thought about the holes he was picking up, and started thinking otherwise. The old Land Rover didn't handle very well, but it was a tank. With a little luck, it might just bring him through.

The sound of several bullets smashing into the windshield brought his mind right back on track. He reached down and picked up his smartphone. Pressing the touch pad for a number stored in memory, he contacted the television studio.

"Hello," a despondent, but friendly voice answered on the other end. "Saul."

"David?" The voice picked up immediately. "Where are you?"

"I'm right on their tail. They seem to be headed south, out-of-town. I'm going to try and stick with them, but I don't know how long I'll be able to keep it up." Saul could hear the bullets hitting the Rover. "These boys really mean business," Hiller continued. "My only hope is that they run out of bullets. See if the Army can set up a roadblock. I'll stay on the horn."

A young soldier was talking on the telephone at the Army command center. His manner was hurried, and no sooner had he hung up, when he rose and ran across the room, shouting as he went.

"Captain, there is a television reporter following them. This is the route they're taking at the moment."

When he reached the captain he handed him a slip of paper. The captain turned to the map of the city hanging on the wall in back of him and studied it for a few seconds, then turned back to the soldier.

"At this point they could be going anywhere. East to Jerusalem or the West Bank, or south to Gaza. I want roadblocks set up for both contingencies. And get the helicopters airborne."

"Yes, sir."

"Hurry!"

The soldier ran back to the desk.

The situation at the television studio was still a mess. People were in a daze, some still weeping, trying to make sense of the affair. Most simply helped the wounded.

Several ambulances arrived and pulled up into the crowd. Medical teams jumped out before the vehicles even came to a stop.

A woman was helping several people to their feet. When that was accomplished, she walked over to where Kaseel lay, reaching down to see if there was any sign of life. She picked up his arm, but something startled her, and she quickly withdrew her hand. Then she reached out and touched the alien once more, noting the different texture of his skin. She slowly turned him over, and as she did so his hood slipped away from his face. She realized immediately that he was not human.

"Over here!" she called out, half in concern, half in fright.

Alerted by the urgency in her voice, a paramedic rushed to her aid. "What is it?"

The woman looked at the body, but did not respond. The paramedic's eyes followed her gaze to the alien. Another paramedic came over to try and speed things up, aware that two people were now staring blankly at a dead body.

"Come on, we've got a lot…" Suddenly, he realized what they were looking at. "What is it?" he said, half turning his head away, yet unable to stop staring out of the corner of his eye.

The road straightened as the terrorists headed southeast out of Tel Aviv. They were now headed toward Jerusalem, but their ultimate goal was to reach the Jordanian border.

Hiller had dropped back as far as he could without losing sight of the terrorists' car. His own vehicle was badly damaged. The radiator was shot out, and steam was pouring from the hood. From the smell, he knew it wouldn't be long before the engine was toast. He prayed for a miracle.

The Israeli response was swift as usual. With Hiller on his cell phone it wasn't long before the choppers had the vehicles in sight. The roadblocks were being pulled into place as quickly as possible, while the helicopters fought a delaying action, blowing up the road in front of the speeding car to slow it down, but not firing on it directly. If there were any way to save the man, they were instructed to do so.

As Basel rounded a bend some ways from the city, he saw that the road was blocked by several Army vehicles, including a tank. He had wondered why the two helicopter gunships had suddenly stopped harassing them. Now he knew. They were hovering in back of the tank, about thirty feet off the deck.

"Roadblock!" Basel yelled to Dace in the back seat.

Hiller saw the roadblock at about the same moment Basel did. The terrorist had brought their car to a screeching halt, and as a result Hiller's Rover ended up a not so discreet distance behind it. He bounced back into his seat, the force of his stop throwing him forward, nearly tipping his vehicle over on its side.

He sat and watched. For several seconds nothing happened. He heard sounds in back of him, and glanced in his rear view mirror. Other Army vehicles had pulled up behind him. They were now blocking all escape routes. Still nothing happened.

"David! What's going on?" Saul's voice crackled over the speaker of Hiller's cell phone.

"So far nothing," Hiller shot back, grabbing the phone off the seat. There was more than a little anxiety in his voice.

Suddenly there was a burst of gunfire, aimed in the direction of the roadblock. The driver's door opened on the terrorists' car and Basel popped out, firing a steady stream of bullets. He was in his glory. He managed to pin the troops down momentarily, and then raced across the road. As he moved away from his vehicle, he turned and fired at Hiller's Land Rover.

"Damn it!" Hiller shouted, as he crunched down in his seat. The bullets rattled around the inside like it was a tin cup.

The gunman nearly made it to the other side before the soldiers manning the roadblock opened fire. In seconds Basel fell to the street, his gun firing into the air until it ran out of bullets. For another few moments all was quiet. Then one of the Israeli officers addressed the remaining terrorists with a loudspeaker.

"Come out of the vehicle with your hands in the air."

Several seconds passed. Nothing happened.

Suddenly the back door of the vehicle was kicked open, and Jesus was shoved out, a belt tightened around his neck. Dace emerged from the back seat right behind him holding the other end. He pulled Jesus toward him savagely, using him as a shield as he leaned back up against the car. Moments later, the woman stepped out as well, with both of them keeping their guns trained on Jesus.

"You let us out of here or I swear I'll kill him!" Dace screamed.

"Let him go," the officer on the loudspeaker responded. "You have no chance of escape. Drop your weapons and lay face down on the ground, hands and feet spread."

"Don't you hear?" the gunman threatened. "I will kill this pig!"

Several marksmen raised their weapons.

Hiller, who was now back up and watching the action, noticed the guns being raised into position. While he had faith in the sharpshooters' abilities, there was something distinctly different at stake here. He whispered to himself, "They'll kill him too."

He leaned out his window to warn the marksmen off when a shot rang out. He saw the woman drop.

"Oh my God!" Hiller was in a panic.

"David, what the hell is going on there?" Saul called out over the cell phone.

Hiller realized that the remaining terrorist could see the sharpshooters now taking aim at him. He didn't panic, but he did act quickly.

In a final, mad thrust of revenge Dace threw Jesus to the ground and opened fire. He ran across the road, spraying the roadblock with bullets, and then turning, fired at his captive.

David leapt from his car, running toward Jesus, shouting.

"No!" Hearing him, the terrorist turned his gun on Hiller who dropped to the ground and covered his head. Sparks from the bullets danced off the pavement.

Several distinct shots rang out from the marksmens' weapons, then all was quiet. The terrorist hit the ground, dead. The last thing to stop moving was his foot.

Hiller stood up, the cellular phone still hanging from his hand. He approached Jesus slowly, tears streaming from his face. But when he got to within a couple of feet, something began to happen.

The body began to glow. It turned blindingly white, like burning magnesium, but without heat. Then the light faded, and with it the body. Within seconds, it had completely vanished.

Hiller stood there, dumbfounded, then slowly brought the cell phone up to his ear.

"My God. He's gone."

"What? Who's gone?" Saul's voice came over the phone, sounding extremely confused.

"The guy they kidnapped," Hiller remarked, still in a fog. "Jesus. He's gone!"

"You mean he escaped?"

"I mean he's—just gone." Hiller dropped the phone to his side.

CHAPTER 41

Even with all the aliens present, life functions was still exceptionally quiet. They were gathered around Jesus as he lay in his stasis chamber. His eyes were closed, and he looked at peace. Liam and Thelis stopped working. They had done everything they could. The best that could be hoped for was that he would be comfortable through to the end.

It had been a horrible scene. All of their worst fears had been realized. There were enough recriminations to go around; if only they had pulled him out sooner; if only Kaseel hadn't gone down. Shafus knew that that kind of speculation was nonproductive, and usually destructive. He knew that Jesus would not want them to feel that way, yet he still found it impossible to keep those feelings at bay.

"You've done all you could," Shafus reassured Liam and Thelis as they put their instruments away. "No one can ask for more."

Jesus' eyes opened slowly. He was relieved to find himself in the safe confines of the alien ship. Even in the haze he was in, he found it ironic that this place, so foreign to him such a short time ago, now seemed like home.

"It is good to see you again," Thelis said, with a glowing smile.

Jesus reached out and touched Thelis' hand. "Good to see you too." A look of alarm flashed across Jesus' face. "Kaseel, is he…"

Shafus put his hand on Jesus' shoulder, and Jesus knew by his touch. "I'm afraid that Kaseel could not be here. I'm sorry."

"Perhaps if I could see him?" Jesus said, trying to rise.

"We weren't able to bring him back. His locator was apparently destroyed by the gunfire." Shafus kept his hand on Jesus until he relaxed back. There was nothing Jesus could do, and Shafus knew he needed to conserve his strength.

"He gave his life for me," Jesus reflected sadly.

"He loved you." Thelis smiled and gave Jesus a reassuring touch.

It was a difficult moment. Wisely, Mance did not allow them to dwell on it. They had been through too much, and had too much yet to go through. "There's nothing more for us here," he said as he looked at the crew, including Jesus in his scan. "It is time to move on."

"We would like you to come with us," Shafus said to Jesus. "Teach us the ways of your Father."

"You already know the ways of my Father, and Earth is where I shall die."

Shafus dropped to his knees. "We're sorry."

"Shafus," Jesus said softly as he reached out and touched the alien's face, "there is purpose in the design. We may not understand it because we see only small pieces of it, but there is a purpose, and we must have faith in that. All of you were right when you said that this was meant to be."

Shafus held his hand and smiled.

Jesus turned his gaze to the others. "My guiding lights to the future. We are different, yet we are one, and you shall always be with me. Always."

Jesus smiled one last time, then closed his eyes. "Thank-you, Father. Thank-you for the gift of these friends." His head fell gently to the side. One-by-one the monitors stopped beeping, and the life-lines went flat, until all was still and silent, except for the low steady drone of the ship.

CHAPTER 42

Three days had passed since Jesus and Kaseel had died, and Mance figured things were about as normal as they would ever be. Time was the only thing that was going to heal this wound, and there was no doubt they had plenty of that.

He was in the control room with Volk, running diagnostics on the hull refit before they ventured back into space. It was essential that they be sure of their work. If it failed while they were at high speed, with everyone in stasis, it would mean death for the entire crew.

"The repair is not perfect, but I believe it will suffice. It's the best I can offer."

"Then it will have to do," Mance said, patting Volk on the shoulder.

"We've also snagged the last time buoy."

"Good. Let everyone know we're ready. We'll meet in the lounge in half an hour and discuss where we go from here."

A half hour later, everyone was present except for Shafus and Thelis. It was traditional for the crew to gather prior to stasis, to work out problems, and make decisions that were of importance to everyone.

On this particular occasion there was an additional matter, the disposition of Jesus' body. Being unable to recover Kaseel had been extremely painful, and not being able to give Jesus a traditional burial was equally difficult. He had been good to them, and launching his body into deep space seemed disrespectful. Then again, it was God's universe.

Liam smiled at Mance who was standing by himself at the front of the ship's lounge. "Well, Mance, anything in mind? Or just point and go?" He knew how badly Mance was feeling, and offered up a little small talk. It would be very important for all of them to be sensitive to each other's needs for some time to come.

"How I would like to go home." Mance sounded so weary.

"Yes," Liam replied.

Thelis entered and sat next to Liam.

While we wait for Shafus," Mance began, confident that Shafus would be along shortly, "I will entertain any feelings you might have regarding Jesus'—burial."

The elevator door opened and Shafus stepped into the lounge. He was very pensive, and remained standing.

Mance continued. "We'll need to decide where, and who will…

"That won't be necessary," Shafus broke in.

"Why?" Thelis asked.

"It's already been taken care of."

He walked over to one of the tables and set something on it. He then unfolded the white linen robe Jesus wore so all could see.

"He's gone."

CHAPTER 43

It was several hours later when the crew assembled in life functions for departure. All preparations were concluded, all checklists complete. While the doctors awoke from stasis before the others, all entered stasis together. The ritual had been in place for as long as the Kels had traveled such incredible distances through space. Their ships had proven themselves over time, but all were aware that each launch presented untold hazards.

As each alien finished stowing his personal belongings, he stood by the side of his stasis chamber. Once everyone was finally ready, Shafus addressed them.

"Our little world," he said as he looked around the room, his voice holding back his emotions, "it has changed forever. Let us think of the families we left so long ago. Let us think about our youngest star, Kaseel, and the qualities he stood for. And let us think of Jesus, who brought us new purpose, and taught us that we will forever be with those we love. Let us say a prayer for Earth and its people. May they hear the voice of the Master as clearly as we have." He paused for only a moment. "Sleep well my friends. God be with you."

The Kels nodded to each other, then climbed into their chambers. After the lids came down, there was a rush of sound as the chambers filled with freezing gas. In an instant the bodies were frozen, and everything was quiet, except for the steady drone of the ship.

Outside, Resurrection's engines ignited in total silence. In seconds, the ship was gone.

EPILOGUE

What was the outcome for Earth? That has yet to be written. For many the enigmatic encounter was a spiritual rebirth. The discovery of the alien body, while answering some questions, created a thousand more. Where did he come from? What part did he play in the encounter with Jesus? The crucifixion? Where was he from?

Many still saw the entire incident as a hoax. They did not believe. Nor did it change their lives, or their spirit.

As for the alien, the authorities were quite satisfied to turn the body over to science, and the military. He would be studied, and the damaged locator found in his arm, analyzed for any military secrets it might reveal.